The Drone Pursuit

TOM SWIFT

INVENTORS' ACADEMY

– BOOK 1 –
The Drone Pursuit

VICTOR APPLETON

Aladdin
NEW YORK LONDON TORONTO SYDNEY NEW DELHI

ALADDIN

An imprint of Simon & Schuster Children's Publishing Division
1230 Avenue of the Americas, New York, New York 10020
First Aladdin hardcover edition July 2019
Text copyright © 2019 by Victor Appleton
Jacket illustration copyright © 2019 by Kevin Keele
TOM SWIFT and related marks are trademarks of Simon & Schuster, Inc.
Also available in an Aladdin paperback edition.
For information about special discounts for bulk purchases, please contact
Simon & Schuster Special Sales at 1-866-506-1949 or business@simonandschuster.com.
The Simon & Schuster Speakers Bureau can bring authors to your live event.
For more information or to book an event contact the Simon & Schuster Speakers Bureau
at 1-866-248-3049 or visit our website at www.simonspeakers.com.
Jacket designed by Heather Palisi-Reyes
Interior designed by Mike Rosamilia
The text of this book was set in Adobe Caslon Pro.
Manufactured in the United States of America 0519 FFG
10 9 8 7 6 5 4 3 2 1
Library of Congress Cataloging-in-Publication Data
Names: Appleton, Victor.
Title: The drone pursuit / by Victor Appleton.
Description: First Aladdin hardcover/paperback edition. | New York : Aladdin, 2019. |
Series: Tom Swift inventors' academy ; #1 | Summary: Tom Swift and his friends at the
Swift Academy work together to retrieve a drone that was taken by the custodian,
Mr. Conway, who they believe is a notorious hacker.
Identifiers: LCCN 2018031887 (print) | LCCN 2018037516 (eBook) |
ISBN 9781534436329 (eBook) | ISBN 9781534436305 (pbk) | ISBN 9781534436312 (hc)
Subjects: | CYAC: Inventors—Fiction. | Drone aircraft—Fiction. | Hackers—Fiction. |
Schools—Fiction. | Friendship—Fiction. | Science fiction.
Classification: LCC PZ7.A652 (eBook) |
LCC PZ7.A652 Dro 2019 (print) | DDC [Fic]—dc23
LC record available at https://lccn.loc.gov/2018031887

Contents

1

The Evasion Equation

THE CAMERA SCANNED THE CROWDED HALLWAY.
A steady stream of students flowed below.

"You will never believe what Deena did this weekend," said a girl's voice.

"What?" asked another girl.

"Her entire family went to . . . ," said the first girl's voice before fading into the clamor of other random voices.

"I think that last one was Ashley Robbins," said Noah. "See if you can get her back."

I adjusted the tiny joysticks on the controller. The view in my visor spun as I rotated our drone to the left.

"Easy, Tom," said Noah. "You're going to make me puke."

"Again," I added. "I warned you about copiloting this mission." Virtual reality can make people nauseated when they're not controlling the movements. And it *always* made my best friend, Noah, more than a little queasy.

Noah Newton and I sat in our algebra classroom wearing VR headsets and earbuds. Meanwhile, our remote-controlled drone hovered in the crowded hallway outside. Now, this may seem weird if we attended any other school—two kids doing a Daft Punk impression twenty minutes before first bell. It may not be grounds for expulsion, but we'd certainly get our virtual reality gear taken away. Things were slightly different here at the Swift Academy of Science and Technology.

It's no big deal to see drones flying above the halls or small robots moving around the students. Last month, Kevin Ryan was out sick with chicken pox and sent a small robot in his place. He had built it with a camera, microphone, and even a converted tablet that showed his pox-covered face on the screen. Kevin wasn't breaking his perfect attendance record no matter how contagious he was. Me, I would've enjoyed the week or two off.

Last week, Mia Trevino created a science experiment that had drifts of snow pouring out of the science lab. I'm talking *real* snow. It gave a whole new meaning to having a snow day at school. So, as you can imagine, the students at the academy have almost seen it all.

"Okay, there," said Noah. "Right there."

I released one of the joysticks and the view on my screen stopped on two girls standing beside an open locker.

"Target acquired," I reported.

"And that was the funniest thing I ever heard," said Ashley's voice in our earbuds.

"Aw, man," said Noah. "We missed it."

Noah and I had spent the entire weekend building a cool surveillance drone. We had modified one of Noah's old drones that came with a small camera on the front. I added an extra camera on the back and three tiny microphones—one on each side and one on the front. And with both of us wearing virtual reality visors, it felt as if we were inside the drone itself. Sure,

VR drones are pretty common. But ours was special for a few reasons.

One thing was my custom-built, tiny parabolic directional microphones. Each one had a tiny dish behind it that focused the sound waves into the microphone. Theoretically, they could not only pick up quality audio from several meters away, but they could also pinpoint and isolate the source of the sound. For example, someone gossiping in a crowded hallway.

Another thing that set our drone apart was the sweet bit of code Noah had written for the onboard audio filters. See, the trouble with having microphones on drones is that they'll always pick up the whirring sound of the four propellers. Well, Noah came up with a cool program that matches the frequency and pitch of each motor and filters out their sound in real time. Now we can hear what the microphones pick up without the motors interfering.

"Bet I can grab it," said a voice in my right earbud.

"Possible hostile," Noah reported. "Three o'clock."

"I'm on it," I said, rotating the drone to the right.

The image spun to the left and Jim Mills came into view. The older, much taller student grew larger in frame as he and his friends walked up the hallway. Jim grinned as he reached a menacing hand toward our drone.

"Dude," said Noah.

I flicked a joystick and our drone zipped to the right, escaping his hand. I adjusted both joysticks to take the drone even higher, out of Jim's reach.

Jim and his friends' laughter sounded in my left earbud as they continued down the hallway.

"Close one," said Noah.

My favorite design innovation was our drone's added maneuverability. I had made some structural changes that gave our drone a nimbleness you don't see in off-the-shelf drones. It also meant that I had spent all of Sunday afternoon perfecting my piloting skills so we could run this test first thing Monday morning.

"Moving back to target," I said pointedly. I rotated the drone back toward Ashley.

BAM!

Ashley slammed her locker shut and walked away with her friend.

"Ow!" Noah and I said in unison. The amplified locker-slam pounded in our earbuds.

"Make a note," said Noah. "Add a sound limiter when we update the software."

I didn't make a note. Instead, I moved one of the joysticks and rotated the drone. "Let's see what else we can . . . uh . . . hear."

"Five minutes until class starts," Noah announced. "Better make it fast."

Hugging the ceiling, the drone drifted down the busy hallway. The twelve- and thirteen-year-old students below bustled from their lockers to their first class. The Swift Academy's best and brightest. Too bad we weren't recording this somehow. The footage would be great for one of my dad's promotional ads.

My father, Tom Swift Sr., created this school from the profits of his company, Swift Enterprises. He built it right next door so kids with an aptitude for science and technology could get a focused education. Sure, we still had to learn the basics, but we also had the freedom and equipment to work on projects beyond the scope of any normal school. Hence the no-big-deal factor of a drone flying through the hallway.

"Aw, man," said Noah.

"What's wrong?" I asked.

"You hear that?" he asked. "I think my audio filter is messing up."

I listened and heard the whirring of drone propellers. The sound grew louder.

"Hang on a minute." I flipped a switch on the controller. A small square appeared in the bottom of my field of view. Just like the picture-in-a-picture feature on a television, this square showed a different camera angle—the rear camera. Another drone sped toward ours from behind. It was a familiar, bright orange drone with flashing blue and red lights.

"Uh-oh," said Noah. "Collybird at six o'clock."

Collin Webb was an older student at the academy who was the first to fly drones through the school. From what I had heard, the teachers weren't that thrilled with the idea. But then Collin volunteered to use his drone as sort of a floating hall monitor. Adding flashing safety lights to his drone, he could hover above the halls and record students who were late for class or catch the occasional student ditching. It became a running joke with the students, as people started saying "Don't let the Collybird see you" or "I would have been here sooner but I had to sneak past the Collybird."

"I can lose him," I said, moving one of the joysticks forward.

The edges of my viewscreen blurred as I piloted the drone faster. It zipped down the long hallway above students' heads. Unfortunately, the Collybird hovered right along after us.

"Not good, Tom," said Noah. "Davenport's straight ahead."

I directed my attention to the end of the long hallway. Our principal, Mr. Davenport, stepped out of a classroom. He stared directly into our camera, his eyes narrowing. He adjusted his glasses and, bald head gleaming, marched toward the approaching drones.

Although our principal didn't mind the occasional drone flying through the halls, I'm guessing a high-speed drone chase would be a different matter.

"Hang on," I said suspendedly. Of course that didn't mean anything since we weren't actually sitting *in* the drone. Still, my body leaned to the left as I veered the drone to the right, where a neighboring wall jolted into view.

"Look out!" said Noah.

Just before hitting the wall, I turned left, making

a wide, arcing U-turn. Instinctively, my body leaned to the right.

"Oh man," groaned Noah. "I think I'm going to hurl."

"Then close your eyes," I said, finishing the turn.

"And miss this?" asked Noah. "Are you kidding?"

I leveled out the drone and flew it straight toward the Collybird. It was a game of drone chicken. "Let's see how much Collin likes his drone."

"Hey, I like *our* drone," said Noah.

The Collybird slowed to a stop and hovered in place. It grew larger on the screen as our drone raced toward it.

"I bet he likes his more," I said.

Just before impact, Collin's drone dropped a foot. Our drone zipped over it and continued down the hallway.

"Whoa," said Noah. "That was close."

"Should buy us some time," I said.

I checked the rear camera and I was right. It took a couple of seconds for Collin to reorient his drone before continuing the chase.

"Tell me you have a plan," said Noah.

"Don't I always?" I asked.

"No," replied Noah. "Not really."

All right, that was fair. Don't you hate it when your friends know you better than you know yourself?

Okay, when it comes to my inventions, I usually make detailed blueprints and schematics before assembling the first two parts together. But when it comes to real-life interactions, I tend to see where the situation takes me. My dad thinks it's my creative side releasing some steam built up from my rigid, analytical side. I don't know if that's true, but it let me off the hook from occasionally annoying him and my friends.

But this time, whether Noah believed it or not, I *did* have a plan.

"It's time to test the new parking mode," I told him.

"Sweet," replied Noah.

I flew the drone to the end of the hallway and out over the open stairwell. I increased power to the rotors and the drone rose. I pulled the right joystick and the drone spun 180 degrees while it continued to rise.

"Oh boy," Noah groaned again.

The approaching Collybird disappeared as our drone rose to the second floor.

When it was high enough, I jammed both joysticks

forward. The drone shot down the new corridor, still hugging the ceiling as before.

I piloted the drone toward the first classroom on the left—Mrs. Gaines's chemistry lab. I didn't fly it into the classroom, though; it hovered just inside the recessed alcove of the entryway. I spun the drone around so the main camera could see the hallway itself. Then I increased power to the motors once more.

Another of my modifications was the set of four thick pins jutting out of the top of the drone. To the casual observer, it may have looked like our drone had four silver antennae, maybe for extra range. Sure, Noah had already extended the control range of our drone, but it had nothing to do with the four pins at the top of the drone. That was my new parking system.

I increased the motor speed further and the drone rose faster. I had to build enough speed so the pins would sink into the foam ceiling tile above. I got the idea one day while watching another student see how many pencils he could get to stick in the ceiling tile before they all fell down on his head.

Eighteen, by the way.

The camera view jostled, and I knew the drone had

hit the ceiling. I slowly powered down the motors to see if the pins had stuck. They had. The drone didn't move at all. I killed the motors completely, but kept the camera on.

Students streamed by in the hallway below. Then the Collybird raced above their heads.

"Yes! We lost him," I said.

I grinned as I powered down the camera and pulled off my visor. I held out a fist to Noah, but he was not in a fist-bumping mood.

Noah removed his visor. A thin rectangular imprint encircled his eyes. But that wasn't the only thing odd about his face. His brown skin was a couple of shades lighter—and a little green.

"I think I'm going to . . ." Noah's eyes widened as he scrambled out of his chair. He pushed past his fellow students as he rushed out of the classroom.

2

The Purloined Prototype

I SHOVED MY VR HEADSET AND CONTROLLER into my backpack. I reached over to Noah's desk and scooped up his gear as well. I put his equipment inside his pack as the classroom began to fill. Mr. Jenkins, our algebra teacher, wasn't the strictest in the school, but if Noah came back late, it wouldn't go well having his desk littered with VR gear.

"Where's Noah?" Amy Hsu asked as she sat at the desk behind his. "He has two minutes and twelve seconds before the bell rings."

Amy didn't look at the clock when she said this. Not

13

only does she have a photographic memory but also an internal clock that I would stack up against any atomic clock in the world.

"He ran to the bathroom," I replied. I thought about sparing Amy the gory details *and* my best bud's honor, but Amy was our close friend. I leaned over and added, "He got sick from our VR drone footage. I think he's yacking his guts out."

Amy's eyes widened in shock. Then she burst into laughter. Her hands shot to her mouth when a small snort escaped.

Even though Amy had been friends with us since the beginning of the school year, she still acted a little shy. It was always fun cracking her up.

"Ew," said Sam's voice behind me. She plopped down at her desk and turned to Amy, who blushed red. "Not the snort, Amy, the yacking part."

Samantha Watson was the last member of the Formidable Foursome, as my dad calls us. Probably the smartest student in the entire school, Sam has never let the G-word ("genius") go to her head.

I quickly recapped our morning drone test and near escape from Davenport and the dreaded Collybird.

"That's your prototype for this month's convention?" asked Amy. She chewed on her lower lip. "Can I see it?"

"It is and I'd love to show you," I replied. "But I had to park it out of sight for now. I'll have to get it after class."

Mr. Edge, our engineering teacher, holds a monthly showcase he calls the "invention convention"—a chance for students to show off their inventing skills. It's pretty informal; we just meet in the cafeteria during lunch. But it's really cool to see all the creative inventions students have been building on the side.

"What about you?" Amy asked Sam. "Are you going to try this month?"

"Same answer as last month, Amy," she replied, running a hand through her short brown hair. "Not going to happen."

Sam actually received a scholarship to the academy for an invention. And it was a big one. She was interviewed on local news channels and even a few national ones. It had something to do with water source engineering. She has always been vague on how it works, since the rights were bought by a company that's currently testing it in a drought-prone nation in Africa. Therefore, Sam has consistently avoided entering the invention conventions. She thinks there's too much pressure to top herself.

Amy glanced at Noah's desk and then up and to the right. I knew this look well. It was as if she was looking at her imaginary internal clock. "Noah has forty-seven seconds left or he's going to be tardy."

I didn't have to check my watch to know that she was spot-on.

Luckily, Noah entered the classroom. His face was no longer pale and its green tint was almost gone. He sighed as he slid into his desk.

"Hey, Amy," he said with a nod. Then he offered a fist bump to Sam. "What up, WG?"

Sam pushed his fist away. "I warned you about that."

Since Sam was somewhat of a celebrity, some of the students nicknamed her "Water Girl." Sam hated that name. So naturally, as her good friends, we had to give her grief about it sometimes.

Sam pushed her glasses up her nose and leaned closer to him, smirking. "I'm going to start calling you HB."

"HB?" Noah asked. "What does that stand for?"

Sam's smirk turned into a full-blown grin. "Hurl Boy."

Amy covered her mouth and giggled.

Noah's eyes widened as he rounded on me. "Dude! I can't believe you told them."

I shrugged. "What are friends for?"

Amy dug into her backpack and rattled through its contents. She finally pulled out a small tin box and handed it to Noah. "Here, have a mint." Amy's backpack was her version of Batman's utility belt.

"Thank you, *Amy*." Noah popped one into his mouth and glared at me. "*That's* what friends are for."

Just then the bell rang. The murmured conversations of the rest of the students faded. Soon there was a class of eager students sitting at their desks, ready to learn algebra. There was just one problem—no teacher.

"Where's Mr. Jenkins?" asked Noah.

I shrugged my shoulders. The rest of the class looked at one another in uncertainty.

After a minute of confused silence, the door opened. A young woman entered with a book and several folders clutched to her chest. She wore thick-framed glasses and her dark hair was pulled up into a small bun.

"Sorry I'm late," she said. She rushed to the head of the class and dropped the folders onto Mr. Jenkins's desk. "I'm Ms. Talbot, your substitute for today."

17

"What happened to Mr. Jenkins?" asked Maggie Ortiz.

Ms. Talbot sighed and dropped into Mr. Jenkins's chair. "He's out sick, I'm afraid." She pointed to the folders on the desk. "And he was kind enough to give me plenty of material to work with." She removed her glasses and rubbed the bridge of her nose. "However, since I was called in at the last minute and haven't had a chance to get up to speed *and* since I expect him back tomorrow ... we're going to do something a little different."

The students glanced around with puzzled expressions. Meanwhile, Ms. Talbot flipped through the file folders.

"If I can just find his log-in info," she muttered.

She finally pulled out a scrap of paper and held it up to her glasses to read it. Then she carefully typed the information into Mr. Jenkins's computer.

"Now, I don't know if there's an exciting documentary about algebra out there," she said. "But I know something that should entertain you little geniuses."

Ms. Talbot tapped a few more keys, and a video streaming web page appeared on the classroom's main board. She selected one of the videos and it began to play.

"Someone get the lights, please," she said.

Terry Stephenson got up from the back row and switched off the classroom lights.

The video's title screen appeared.

"The Ten Most Notorious Hackers in History," Sam read.

"Cool," said Noah. "I've seen this one." He put his head on his desk. "Total nap time."

Who could blame him? He had just been sick, after all. Besides, Noah probably knew every famous hacker by heart. He was a huge programming geek.

The documentary was interesting. It began with one of the first hackers ever—John Draper, who was nicknamed Cap'n Crunch. He was the guy who used the toy whistle from a box of Cap'n Crunch cereal to hack the telephone system.

The video went on to list other famous hackers. Some of them hacked into NASA, looking for UFO evidence. Others had hacked into major corporations, stealing credit card information. The FBI had caught most of them. Some of them had even been convinced to use their skills for good. They called themselves "white-hat hackers." However, a couple of them were still at large.

Hacking and programming have never really been my thing, so I spent most of the time sketching out another drone design. Don't get me wrong, I'm a decent programmer, enough to get good grades in computer language classes. But I've never had the passion or talent for it like Noah has.

I felt a nudge on my back. "Who does that guy look like?" Sam whispered.

I looked up at the video and saw a black-and-white photograph of a man with light hair and thick side-burns.

I shrugged. "I don't know. Elvis?"

Sam nudged me harder. "No. Doesn't that look like Mr. Conway?"

Mr. Conway was the school's custodian. He was much older than the man in the photograph, had gray hair, and didn't have sideburns. He did have a similar pointed nose, as well as a stocky frame. It was hard to tell, since the photograph showed the man in profile and he wore lightly tinted sunglasses.

"I can see the resemblance," I said. "Kinda."

"I totally see it," whispered Amy.

The video went on to identify the hacker only by his online username: Sh4dow H4wk—he did that weird programmer thing where he replaced some of the letters with numbers. Shadow Hawk's true identity was never discovered, since he was never caught. He supposedly hacked into several military and government agency servers.

"If Shadow Hawk is still on the FBI's Most Wanted list, I bet there's a big reward for his capture," said Sam.

When Shadow Hawk's photo came up on the video again, Amy gently nudged Noah.

"Wha-what?" asked a groggy Noah.

Amy pointed at the screen. "Doesn't that look like Mr. Conway?" she whispered.

Noah squinted at the video. "Maybe. When he was younger." He grinned. "Check out those sideburns."

"Sam and Amy think Mr. Conway is some fugitive hacker," I whispered.

Noah was taken aback. "What? No, not Mr. Conway. I like him." He nudged me. "Remember that time he came up with a perfect solvent for our ... uh ... mishap?"

Of course I remembered. The entire school remembered how our automated street painter went off during transport. Noah and I, along with three innocent bystanders and three square meters of school hallway, were blasted with the soothing shade of bright safety orange. Lucky for us, Mr. Conway had mixed a cleaner that removed the orange paint without damaging school property.

Our prototype didn't make it to the convention that month.

"That means he's smart," Sam concluded. "That doesn't mean he wasn't a hacker when he was younger."

Noah looked back at the video. "Really? Naw. Can't be."

The video moved on to the next famous hacker and we continued to bicker quietly until we were shushed by Ms. Talbot. We went back to watching the video while she went back to typing on Mr. Jenkins's computer.

Sam's theory didn't really surprise me. She was something of an amateur conspiracy theorist. The four of us would often have discussions about the existence of Bigfoot or captured aliens at Area 51. Sam would always take the side of the implausible. As intelligent as she was, she felt it was more fun believing in fantastic things and then theorizing about the science of how they could exist. Honestly, she got a little carried away sometimes.

The video ended just before the bell rang. I packed my backpack so I could be the first one out.

"What's the hurry, Tom?" asked Sam.

"I have to grab the drone before someone finds it," I replied.

"You need help?" asked Noah.

I shook my head. "It's on my way."

"You should be okay," said Noah. "Mrs. Gaines usually has the class cleaning beakers and putting away chemicals well into the break."

He was right. I should be able to work in the doorway without being run over by escaping students.

"That used to drive me nuts." Amy shook her head. "Always threw me off schedule."

When the bell rang, I was the first one out the door. I jogged down the hallway and raced up the steps. The halls would fill quickly and I still didn't know how I was going to get the drone off the ceiling tiles. I might have to borrow a stool from the chemistry lab. Actually, I would probably have to haul the stool through a rush of students, and *then* have someone keep people from coming out of the class while I climbed up to get the drone. It would be easier if I got there before the next group of kids was filing into the classroom, too.

I made it to the top of the stairs and headed toward the chem lab. I got to the doorway, looked up, and . . .

The drone was gone.

3

The Basement Abasement

MY FIRST THOUGHT WAS THAT THE PINS HADN'T
held and the drone had crashed to the floor during first
period. I scanned the floor, expecting to see bits of broken drone everywhere—however, the floors were clean.
It hadn't crashed and someone hadn't simply cleaned
up the pieces, either. There wasn't a trace of the drone
anywhere.

That meant someone had taken our drone from the
ceiling.

I scanned the hallway. Students poured from classroom doors, but no one seemed to be watching me, waiting for a reaction. I almost wished I *had* seen someone like that. At that moment, I would've loved to have been on the receiving end of some sort of prank.

Ha, ha. Very funny. You got me. Now . . . can I have my drone back, please?

With no pranksters in sight, I left the doorway and drifted into the flow of foot traffic. I tried to reason out the possibilities. Maybe we didn't lose the Collybird after all. Maybe Collin's drone doubled back and spotted ours. If he came back himself and took it down, then that meant he would've reported us to Principal Davenport. Of course, Mr. Davenport wouldn't know it was our drone until we tried to claim it.

Perfect. So, if we claim the drone, we get in trouble. If we *don't* claim it, then we lose our prototype for the invention convention. Noah was going to kill me.

I adjusted the weight of my backpack and moved farther down the hallway. Then I remembered why my pack was heavier than usual. I still had my VR gear.

That was it!

I quickened my pace and searched for a secluded area. The library was halfway down the corridor and I ducked inside. Luckily, Mrs. Welch was with a student at the front desk so she didn't see me come in. I darted between two bookshelves and crouched. I had my VR headset turned on in a flash and powered up the drone's cameras. If I couldn't see our drone, then at least I could see what our drone saw.

My VR screen came to life and I saw kids walk past the camera. The drone was in one of the hallways as students rushed to class. I exhaled with relief. At least I didn't see the inside of Mr. Davenport's office on the screen. Whoever had taken our drone was still on the move.

I switched on the drone's rear camera but the screen was black. The lens must've been blocked by something, maybe by whoever was holding it.

I breathed a sigh of relief. There was still hope that I could get our drone back without dealing with Davenport, Collin, or anyone else who had the power to confiscate our prototype. I just had to figure out where it was.

I toggled back to the front camera and tried to get a clue of who had it. I couldn't see any part of the person. They just walked along the crowded hallway. In fact, whoever had the drone walked very smoothly.

The image on the screen moved so steadily that it was almost as if the drone was flying. But since the angle of the video was askew, I knew that couldn't be the case.

I turned my attention to the drone's surroundings. Unfortunately, between the mass of students and the fact that all of the classrooms looked the same from the outside, I couldn't tell where in the school it was. It could be on any of the three floors.

I groaned with frustration. My newfound hope evaporated faster than a cube of dry ice in hot water.

My thumbs instinctively moved to the joysticks as if I could turn the drone to get a better look around. But with the drone powered down, I was at the mercy of whoever was holding it. If I started the drone now, I risked damaging it if the person dropped it in surprise. I sighed and continued to scan the surroundings for a clue, *any* kind of clue that gave me the drone's location.

Then I knew exactly where it was.

Between passing students, I had caught a glimpse of BB-8. Mrs. Scott has a poster featuring the popular *Star Wars* droid on the door of her robotics class. Whoever had the drone was on the third floor.

"Yes!" I said to myself.

I raised my headset to my forehead and bolted out of the library. I made my way through the crowded hallway toward the stairs at the end.

I heard a "Nice hat, Swift," and even a "Take me to your leader," but I ignored the jabs and kept moving.

I took the stairs two at a time until I was on the third-floor landing. Then I made my way to Mrs. Scott's robotics class. I slid to a stop in front of BB-8 and bent over to catch my breath. I glanced around but didn't see anyone holding our drone.

I slipped down the headset. The viewscreen showed the end of the hallway. My stomach lurched a bit when the view swung around. Whoever had the droid had just turned left.

I was closing in!

I slid up the headset and dashed down the hall. The crowd was thinning as the time for the next bell approached. I was probably going to be late for second period but I would deal with that later. I quickened my pace. Whatever trouble I had to talk my way out of would be worth it if I could just find out who had swiped our drone.

I made it to the end of the hall and turned left. The

entrance to the stairs was to the right. The only thing to the left was the service elevator, and the only person there was Mr. Conway. The short, balding man had his back to me as he pushed his cleaning cart onto the waiting elevator car. I looked past him and saw our drone resting on his cart.

"Mr. Conway!" I shouted as I ran toward the elevator.

He didn't seem to hear me. Instead of turning he reached over and pushed a button on the elevator without looking out of the car. The doors began to close.

I made it to the doors just after they shut. I punched the call button several times, but I was too late.

I glanced up, but the service elevator didn't have any kind of directional indicator above it, like some elevators. I didn't know which floor Mr. Conway was headed for. I sighed and lowered my visor. I was definitely going to be late for class.

The viewscreen showed the interior of the elevator for a while. Then the view shifted. Mr. Conway pulled the cart out of the elevator. I looked around for any clue to his location. I didn't recognize anything at first. It didn't look like the rest of the school. Then the stairwell came into view. There were stairs leading to the level above, but there were no stairs leading down. Mr. Conway was in the basement.

I raised my visor and sprinted for the stairs. With everyone else in class by now, I could really fly down the steps. Down to the first floor and then down to the basement.

I always knew there was a basement in the school but I never had reason to go down there before. As far as I knew, it was mostly storage. Occasionally, a teacher would talk about digging something out of the basement. Want to show a video that's only available on an old VHS tape? We'll have to get a VCR out of the basement. Looking for a chart of the solar system that still includes Pluto as a planet? Basement.

I came off the last step to find myself in a dimly lit alcove. Several cardboard boxes were stacked in corners and shoved under the stairs. A flickering fluorescent bulb gave the area a creepy, horror-movie kind of feel. If any of the students had bothered to come into the basement, there could totally be some cool rumors about former students being locked up down here, or other spooky stuff. I made a mental note to tell Noah so we could get right on that.

Up ahead, Mr. Conway pushed his cart through an open doorway. A long hallway led beyond.

"Excuse me," I said. "Mr. Conway?"

Once again, he didn't turn. Instead, Mr. Conway rolled his cart through the doorway and the door swung closed behind him.

I ran up to the door and grabbed the handle to pull it open. The door didn't budge. I pulled harder but it was locked tight. I glanced left and saw a gray plastic box and keypad mounted on the wall beside the door. A tiny red light blinked on the upper left corner of the box. Mr. Conway must've used a key card or a code to get through.

I knocked on the door's large glass window. "Mr. Conway," I said louder.

He ignored me once again. He kept pushing his cart down the hallway beyond.

That's when I noticed the tiny white cables stretching from his overalls pocket. They split and one cable went to each of the custodian's ears. Mr. Conway was listening to music on his phone or some kind of MP3 player.

And then the bell rang.

Great. I was late for nothing.

4

The Search Suppression

"OH, DUDE," SAM SAID BETWEEN BITES OF HER apple. "Noah is going to be so mad."

I hadn't had a chance to tell anyone about the drone abduction all morning. My friends and I had different classes after first period. And in the ones we did have together, we couldn't get away with whispering to each other. I had to wait until I saw everyone at lunch.

"It's not like I lost the thing," I said. I mindlessly twirled my mashed potatoes with a plastic spork. "I mean, okay, it's kinda my fault. But I know where it is now."

Sam laughed. "Held hostage by the hacker-in-hiding, Mr. Conway."

"You still on that Conway thing?" Noah asked. He set down his food tray and sat. Amy was right behind him.

"Oh . . . he's definitely a person of interest." Sam looked at me with a glint in her eye.

"What did you find out?" Amy asked Sam. "I've been thinking about that movie all morning. I haven't had a chance to do any research yet. But did you?"

"It's not the hacking thing," I said. Then I went on to tell Amy and Noah about the fate of our drone. As I relayed the story, I watched Noah's expressions rise and fall with each turn. As I wrapped it up, his face cemented in a grimace.

Noah slowly shook his head. "Man, I'm so mad at you right now."

Sam smirked at me. "Told you."

Noah pointed at me. "You do the invention convention all the time, but this is my first one! I even donate one of my drones to the cause and now it's gone?"

"I know, I know," I said, raising both hands. "But don't worry, I'll get it back. I'll just catch Mr. Conway and ask for it. Simple as that."

Noah snorted. "If he doesn't turn it in to Mr. Davenport first."

"If he was going to do that, he probably would've done it already," Sam said between bites. "Instead of taking it all the way to the basement."

"To the *locked* basement," Amy added. "What does he really want with your drone, huh?" She glanced around and then leaned forward. "I wonder what he's *really* doing down there."

"Custodian stuff," I replied. "What else?"

"With a security keypad?" asked Amy. "Why such a highly secure area for a school basement?"

"I saw one keypad," I said. "That's it. That hardly makes it Fort Knox."

Sam popped a cherry tomato into her mouth. "Conway could be hacking into more government agencies as we speak." She gave a sly grin. "The basement could be his secret lair."

I laughed, nearly choking on my food. "Who says 'lair'?"

Noah sighed with frustration. "This is crazy. Mr. Conway is not that Shadow Hawk guy." He crossed his arms and leaned back in his seat. "There's no way some world-famous hacker is hiding out in our school."

I glanced around and cringed when I saw other students taking notice of our conversation. Barry Jacobs craned his neck to get a better look from his table.

"Uh, I think we should keep it down," I whispered. "You want everyone knowing about this?"

"Uh, yeah," Sam said. "What if we're right?" She leaned forward and jutted a thumb at Amy. "I trust Amy's photographic memory." Then she lowered her voice. "And if she thinks Conway looks like Shadow Hawk, then I agree with her. It's at least worth checking out."

Amy dug out her phone. "Wow. Okay, that's a lot of pressure on me now." She pulled up her web browser. "Maybe there's more information on the FBI's website."

Sam and I gathered around Amy as she pulled up a page. The same black-and-white photo appeared on the FBI's site. But this time, they also listed Shadow Hawk's approximate characteristics.

"He has blond hair," Sam read. "No help there. Mr. Conway's hair is gray."

Amy zoomed in on the hacker's height. "Look. It says he's about five three. Mr. Conway is about that height."

Noah rolled his eyes. "Because there are no other

hackers who are five three." He took another bite from his sandwich.

After I saw the photo again, and after just running into Mr. Conway, I had to admit, they did look a lot alike. More than I thought the first time I saw the photo.

"Pull up a photo of Mr. Conway," Sam said. "Maybe we can compare them side by side." She grinned up at Noah and me. "If there is a photo of Conway on the web, Amy can find it. She's a search master."

"Good idea," said Amy. "I think his first name is Joshua."

I stood up and stretched. "Let's go to the computer lab and do this," I suggested. "So we don't have to crowd around Amy's phone."

"You really buying into this?" Noah asked me.

I rubbed the back of my neck. "I don't know. Maybe." I sat back in my chair. Sam and Amy are two of the smartest students here. If they believed it, I thought it was worth looking into. Besides, we still had twenty minutes left of lunch period.

Noah shrugged. "All right. Let's do some digging and rule this out so we can concentrate on getting our drone back."

We finished our lunch and zipped over to the nearby computer lab. Everyone was still in the cafeteria during the rest of the lunch period, so we had the place to ourselves. Amy logged on to one of the computers and the rest of us pulled up chairs. We could've all searched on different computers, but Sam was right. Amy whizzed through the search engine and different social media sites faster than our eyes could keep up.

"This is weird," Amy said. "I'm not getting any information about Mr. Conway."

"Really?" asked Sam.

Noah sighed. "Let me try something." He slid his chair over to the next computer. He tapped the space bar, and the screen saver was replaced with the school's log-in page. Noah logged in and pulled up the Swift Academy's official website. He clicked through a couple of pages. "That's weird. He's not listed in the staff section," Noah reported. "They have everyone else's picture there."

Amy's fingers blurred over the keyboard as she typed. "Nothing on social media. Nothing on phone listings. Nothing relevant with Josh or J. Conway. I'm drawing a blank."

"That is too weird," I said. How can anyone manage

not to leave some kind of digital footprint these days? It would certainly take mad hacking skills to erase any trace of someone from the Internet. Could Sam really be onto something this time?

I glanced up at Sam. She looked back at me and shrugged. Then we both grabbed computers of our own and began to search.

"Nothing with an image search," Sam reported.

"Zilch on class reunion sites," added Noah.

"I'm working local census records," I said.

"I was just getting to that," said Amy. "What did you find?"

I typed a few more keys. "Nothing," I replied.

This was too strange. Here we were, four of us burning up the Internet, searching for any trace of Mr. Conway, and we weren't finding anything. It was as if the man didn't exist. But then, something stranger happened.

All four of our computers shut down at once. In fact, *all* of the computers in the computer lab went dark. The dancing geometric shape screen savers all disappeared in unison. Every computer screen was black. We glanced around at one another in disbelief.

"Okay," said Noah. "That's . . . something."

5

The Communication Complication

PING.

My phone chimed as I received a text.

I got up from my desk and walked toward my bedroom door. I stepped on the pressure pad just inside my room and the robotic arm on my bedside table extended toward me. The plastic hand opened, revealing my phone resting in its palm. I unplugged the phone from the tiny power jack jutting from the plastic wrist. You know, with just a few weeks designing, a 3D printer, and a trip to a Halloween store, I never had to search my room for my phone. It was simply offered to me as I left. It wasn't really invention convention material, but it kept me from forgetting my phone.

My room was a mess of inventions like that. Actually, to the casual observer, my room was just a mess. Okay, maybe to the astute observer, too. But hey, I have a very complex and detailed *pile* system. I can find any book, note, or schematic in any of the many piles around my room. Really. My dad didn't always agree with my system. He had me clean my room once and I was lost for months. We finally met halfway. As long as there were no dirty dishes and the dirty clothes stayed in the hamper, I was golden.

I sat on my bed and checked my phone. The text was from Noah. **What are we going to do?**

I wasn't sure if he meant our missing drone or the Conway situation. But my answer was the same for both.

My thumbs flew across my phone screen. **Don't worry. We'll figure it out.**

None of us had a chance to talk after the big computer blackout. At first, we thought it was just the computers in the computer lab that went down. It turned out that every computer in the entire school went out. I

41

didn't realize just how much our school relied on computers until we couldn't use them at all.

The students weren't the only ones taking computers for granted. The teachers used them for electronic slide shows, pulling examples from the Internet, and even making notes digitally on the electronic boards in front of each class. The afternoon classes were a little chaotic to say the least.

Teachers dug out old dry-erase boards and overhead projectors (the ones with bulbs that still worked). Even the school bell system was offline. Individual classes dismissed according to the classroom clocks. And since the clocks weren't synchronized, class beginning and ending times were staggered throughout the school.

Ping.

You don't really think Mr. Conway crashed the computers, do you? Noah asked in his next text. **Because we were looking into him?**

The timing is pretty suspicious, I replied.

He doesn't seem like the kind of person who would do something like that, Noah wrote.

Unless he was a wanted hacker trying to cover his tracks, I thought. Instead, I wrote: **You're right. He doesn't.**

"Tom," my dad called from downstairs. "Dinner's ready."

Gotta go, I typed. **Talk to you tomorrow**. I slipped the phone into my pocket and went downstairs.

My dad had the table set and a freshly cooked meat loaf ready to go. I had to hand it to him. For someone who runs a major tech company with massive government contracts, he always makes time to have dinner with me every night. Since my mom died when I was little, he has always tried to be two parents in one. Luckily, being his own boss lets him set his own hours and even work from home when he wants.

"Heard you had an interesting day at school today," he said.

I froze mid-bite. Was he talking about our lost drone? Had someone told him about our Conway investigation? Tom Swift Sr. knew about everything that went on in Swift Enterprises. It would make sense that he would keep his ear to the ground at the next-door Swift Academy. I mean, when they both have your name on them, you kind of have to.

"The computer outage?" my dad asked. He chuckled. "Surely you noticed."

I laughed, mostly with relief. "Oh, yeah. It was crazy."

I told him about the teachers scrambling to find low-tech solutions to replace their new high-tech problem.

"Mr. Wilkins seemed happy about the whole thing," I said. "He thinks we rely too much on technology. He said it was a good chance for the teachers to stretch *their* brains for a change."

"I'm sure he has a point there," my dad said. "Still, we're sending in someone to fix things. We think someone uploaded a virus into the system."

"Oh yeah?" I said. "Do you know who it was?" I asked.

You don't have to be a world-famous hacker to upload a virus to a computer system. Then again, a world-famous hacker could probably do it with ease . . . and not get caught.

"No, and that's not the priority right now," my dad replied. "We need to clean the virus as soon as possible. After all, the academy's servers are tied to Swift Enterprises. There are firewalls in place, but you never know."

That was news to me and I mentally kicked myself for not thinking of it sooner. Of course there was a link between the Swift Academy and Swift Enterprises (other than the name). But I didn't know their computer systems were linked somehow. Suddenly the meat loaf felt like a rock in my stomach.

"Do you think someone was trying to hack into the company's servers?" I asked.

My dad shrugged. "I doubt it. It was probably just an overzealous student. Wouldn't be the first time."

My father seemed way too nonchalant about the whole thing. But *if* Mr. Conway was really Shadow Hawk and *if* he got a job at the academy to be closer to Swift Enterprises and *if* he released the virus . . . then this *was* a big deal. I opened my mouth to tell my dad about our suspicions. But then I closed it again. There was one problem—way too many ifs.

I couldn't go to my dad with some half-baked conspiracy theory. He's warned me about having too many side interests as it is. He thinks I don't apply myself enough at school. Sure, I make decent grades and all. And sure, if I concentrated more I could probably ace all my classes. The trouble is, I like exploring everything and get excited about some new idea or invention. My dad would think this Conway investigation was just another distraction. He wouldn't take it seriously. We needed more than just a theory.

Ping.

I pulled out my phone when it chimed again. It was probably Noah.

I opened my messages to a text from an unknown number.

Back off, it read.

That was weird. Must've been a wrong number or something. Or maybe one of my friends got a new phone and was updating his or her contacts.

Strange way to announce a new phone purchase, though.

I quickly typed a reply. **Who is this?**

There was no response.

"No phones at the table, Tom," my dad said.

"Sorry," I replied, slipping the phone back into my pocket.

My dad and I finished dinner. We talked more about my day and his day—what he could tell me that wasn't top secret. But honestly, I don't remember our conversation. My mind kept going back to the Conway conspiracy and that strange text.

6

The Surveillance Solution

"BACK OFF?" ASKED SAM. "IT'S *GOTTA* BE Conway. He's onto us."

"Us?" I asked. "Did you get a text too?"

"No," Sam replied.

I turned to Amy and Noah. "What about you two?"

They shook their heads. "Looks like you're the only one," said Amy.

Sam shrugged. "Okay. Looks like he's onto you, Tom."

As everyone showed up for first period, I told my friends about my conversation with my dad. I told them how the school's servers are connected to my dad's company. And I ended everything with the mysterious text.

Amy kneaded her hands together. "Did you tell your father any of this?"

I shook my head. "But maybe I should. I don't know."

"What I want to know is: How are we going to get our drone *now*?" asked Noah. "If Conway's onto you, then you can't ask for it back." He pointed to himself. "And he knows we're buds, so that leaves me out."

I shushed Noah and glanced around the classroom. Students were filing in, and Noah wasn't being quiet. Kaylee Jackson and Barry Jacobs pointed and whispered.

I didn't have to answer Noah. The bell rang—the usual bell. Unlike the afternoon before, we didn't have to wait for the teacher to keep time. Of course, that would've been difficult in this case because, like yesterday, we didn't have a teacher.

"Good morning, Swift Academy students," said Mr. Davenport's voice over the loudspeaker. "As you can see, the bell and intercom systems are working again. However, the computer and wireless Internet systems are still offline. It turns out our system was infected with a computer virus . . . again."

Mr. Davenport had to be referring to last year's big April Fool's prank. Everyone called it the computer *cat*-astrophe because every computer in the entire school played an endless loop of funny cat videos from around the Internet. It only lasted for an hour and I heard Anya Latke got in big trouble for pulling it off. But to the academy students, she was a hero.

"Now we all had a little chuckle from the last time," Davenport continued, "but this virus is quite malicious. We have someone coming in to take a look but until then, we're going to have to make do a little longer. Thank you."

Suddenly, the door flew open and Ms. Talbot swept into the classroom. "Sorry I'm late again." She carried an armload of folders and a large satchel to the front. "It turns out that Mr. Jenkins has a bout of food poisoning." She held up a hand. "He'll be fine, but he'll probably be out for the rest of the week." She put her things down on the desk. "Which means that I'll actually have to teach some real algebra."

She rummaged through her satchel. "Unfortunately, all of Mr. Jenkins's lesson plans are on the school computer system. So . . . we're going to watch another movie today."

Sighs of relief rippled throughout the class. Several students began slipping their phones and books from their backpacks.

Amy raised a timid hand. "Excuse me," she said. "But how are you going to show a movie if the computers are down?"

Ms. Talbot pulled a laptop out of her bag. "I brought my own computer." She took out some other cables and devices. "And a wireless hotspot to access the Internet through my phone." She gave the class a grin. "And no, you can't have the password."

While Ms. Talbot connected her computer to the system, Noah leaned over. "Whatever is going on with Mr. Conway, we have to get that drone back," he said. "This was just a test flight. You were going to calibrate the microphones, I was going to tweak the filter program. We have tons of work to do to be ready on Friday. We should just go ask him for it."

Sam leaned over. "Want to know my opinion?" she asked.

"If it means not getting our drone back, then no," said Noah.

Sam rolled her eyes. "Mr. Conway has your drone somewhere in the basement, right?"

"Yeah," I agreed.

"And we want to know what he's up to, right?" Sam asked.

"Yeah," I replied.

Amy's eyes widened. "Then why not just turn on the cameras and see what he's doing?"

Like I said, two of the smartest students at the academy.

7

The Power Predicament

THE FOUR OF US DECIDED TO SKIP LUNCH AND
see what the drone could see in the basement. Noah
and Sam scouted the school for Mr. Conway while
Amy and I went down to the basement itself.

Everyone thought Amy would be the best copilot
not only because of her photographic memory, but also
because Noah got sick during the last flight. Nothing
like someone running to the bathroom to ruin a covert
operation.

Once at the end of the stairs, we couldn't get through
the basement's main access door, but we had to get as

close as possible so the remote and headsets would definitely be in range. Amy and I slid under the stairs and pulled a couple of the cardboard boxes in front of us. Once we were hidden, we put the visors on.

"No sign of him yet," came Noah's voice in my ear. I had an earpiece attached to my phone. Amy had one too. She was in contact with Sam.

"Okay, let's see what we can see," I said as I hit a switch on the controller.

The screen on my headset turned on but it barely glowed.

"Did you turn it on yet?" asked Amy.

"I did," I replied. "I think the drone's in a room with the lights out."

"Or something could be covering the camera," said Noah, listening in on our conversation.

"I don't think so," I said. "There's a dim glow coming from the bottom of the screen. And I see a bunch of green dots."

"I see them too," said Amy. "I thought maybe something was wrong with the camera."

"The camera better be okay," Noah warned.

"I'm going to see if I can get a better view," I said.

I moved the left joystick, powering up the drone's motors. I just hoped the drone wasn't parked next to anything that could get entangled with the propellers. If it was, this was going to be a very short spy mission. And Noah was definitely going to kill me.

The dim view shifted as the drone rose a couple of inches into the air. The green dots danced around on the screen as the drone evened out. I adjusted the other joystick to move it forward, before a bright light suddenly blinded me.

"Ah!" I cried out.

Amy gasped. "Someone turned on the lights."

I rotated the drone to the right. It hovered in a small room with a single door leading out and a small closet on the side. There wasn't a standard light switch on the wall beside the main door. Instead, there was a white plate with a small plastic dome.

"What's going on?" asked Noah.

"Motion-sensor switch," I replied. "The drone must've triggered it."

"Sam says she spotted Mr. Conway," Amy reported. "Third floor, next to engineering."

"Good," I said. "At the other end of the school."

I rotated the drone some more and saw where it had been parked. A large metal shelving unit extended across one wall. The drone had been on a pile of dark cloths on one of the shelves.

"Any motion sickness, Amy?" I asked.

"I'm good," she replied.

"Amy says she's all good, Noah," I said a little louder.

"Oh, sure," said Noah in my earpiece. "Ask her after some of your crazy flying-through-the-halls action."

"What is that blinking red light at the bottom of the screen?" asked Amy.

I hissed with surprise. I was so focused on the room that I hadn't noticed. A red dot slowly flashed at the bottom right corner of the viewscreen.

"We're almost out of juice," I replied. "That's the low-battery light."

"We better hurry, then," said Amy.

I scanned the shelves and saw nothing out of the ordinary. Basically, the shelves were full of nothing particularly sinister, just stuff you'd expect to find in a custodian's storeroom in the basement. There were a couple of toolboxes, office supplies, and rows of plastic jugs that looked as if they contained industrial cleaning solutions. You know, stuff that's probably safer locked away from students who enjoy experimenting with various chemicals.

"Sam says Mr. Conway is heading toward the elevator," Amy reported.

I didn't reply. Instead I rotated the drone more and discovered the source of the light we had seen earlier.

"I think we have something," I said.

"What is it, Tom?" asked Noah.

A computer monitor and keyboard sat on a small desk. The monitor ran the same screen saver as those in the computer lab—colorful geometric shapes bouncing through black space.

"He has a computer down here," I replied.

"Is it tied into the school?" asked Noah. "If it is, how is it even running?"

"That's not all that's down here," said Amy. "Turn the drone to the right, Tom."

"On it," I said as I nudged the joystick.

The view slowly shifted. Beside the computer desk were rows and rows of computer servers. The green dots we saw in the darkness were the tiny power lights on each individual hard drive. Multicolored cables connected them to each other. The unit nearly reached to the ceiling and the drives were in four rows, stacked eight deep.

"Whoa," I whispered.

"Uh . . . Sam says Mr. Conway is *in* the elevator," Amy reported.

"I'm heading to the second floor to see if he gets out there," announced Noah.

I hardly paid attention to what my friends said. I was too amazed by what I saw. I couldn't believe that Mr. Conway had access to the entire school's server farm. This system would not only back up every computer in the school but also power the entire school intranet. If Conway truly was Shadow Hawk, it would be no big deal for him to hack into the system. He could do it so easily, anytime he wanted and in complete privacy. But if that were the case, then why would he need the virus?

"He didn't get out on the second floor," Noah reported. "I'm going down to the first."

"Sam thinks Mr. Conway is on his way down," said Amy. When I didn't reply, Amy bumped my shoulder. "Did you hear me, Tom?"

My mind was still running through different scenarios.

Did Conway just want to crash the system for some reason? Maybe he needed to introduce the virus to keep the system busy so he couldn't be detected hacking into Swift Enterprises.

"Tom?" Amy nudged me again. "Mr. Conway is coming. You have to put the drone back where it was, so he doesn't suspect anything."

"Oh, yeah. I will," I replied. I turned the drone back to the computer. "I just want to check something first."

"What?" asked Amy.

"He didn't get out on the first floor," Noah buzzed in my ear. "He's coming to you."

"What are you doing?" Amy squeaked.

I lowered the drone. "If I can bump a key on the keyboard, it'll shut off the screen saver. Then we can see what he's working on."

Noah heard my plan. "What if Conway sees a drone hovering over the computer?" asked Noah. "What happens then, huh?"

I piloted the drone closer to the keyboard. I had to be careful to just tap one of the keys with one of the drone's landing struts. If I hit it with too much force, I could lose control of the drone and crash it. The battery light blinked faster at the bottom of the screen. I was running out of power.

I heard the elevator doors open.

"He's here," Amy whispered.

I knew that Mr. Conway couldn't see us hidden under the stairs, so I wasn't worried about getting caught that way. But I knew I was running out of time, too.

"Park the drone where you found it, Tom," Noah ordered. "He's gotta be down there by now."

I didn't reply. Instead, I edged the drone closer to the keyboard. The battery light flashed faster. I just needed a little more time.

I heard the basement security door open and shut.

"He's through the door and going down the hallway," said Amy. "He's going to see the drone."

I was out of time.

8

The Persuasion Situation

I GROWLED IN FRUSTRATION. I PUSHED UP ON the joystick, leaving the keyboard be. Now I just had to make it back to the shelf before Mr. Conway entered. The drone rose and then rotated away from the computer. The battery light flashed in the corner as I tried to concentrate on flying. I tried to rotate as fast as possible without losing control or overshooting my destination. As the entry door came into view, I saw it crack open. I spotted Mr. Conway's hand on the doorknob as the door began to swing in.

I wasn't going to make it.

Tap-tap-tap-tap!

Something made a loud noise beside me. I peeked out from under my headset and saw Amy at the security door. She tapped on the glass with one of her rings.

I turned my attention back to the drone's camera. The storeroom door closed. Amy had bought me some more time. I moved the joystick forward and took the drone higher. I flew it into the shelving unit and rotated it around. Maybe I could park it in such a way that the camera would be aimed at the computer. That way we could at least see what Mr. Conway was up to later.

I heard him open the main security door.

"Hi, Mr. Conway," Amy said.

"Hello, Amy," he replied. "What are you doing down here?"

"Well, uh . . . first we looked for you on the third floor," she replied. "But you weren't there. So then we checked the second floor and then the first floor. But we didn't check the basement. But that's where you are. Down here in the basement."

Amy tended to ramble when she was nervous. But I think she was also trying to stall him.

I didn't let her effort go to waste. I took the time to

get the drone's camera angle just right. The computer screen was in view and, from my new angle, it wouldn't be blocked by whoever sat in front of the keyboard.

Mr. Conway laughed. "Well, you found me. Your quest is at an end, young lady. Now, what do you need?"

Amy laughed nervously. "Uh, okay . . . uh . . . yes. What do I need? That's the question. The one you just asked me. The question I need to answer."

Oh boy. She was just plain rambling at this point.

"Amy?" asked Mr. Conway.

"There's been a spill in the cafeteria," she blurted out.

Mr. Conway chuckled. "Well, don't worry. These things happen. I'll be right up to take care of it," he replied. "Oh, and Amy?"

"Yes, sir?" she asked.

"They got the intercom up and running," he said. "No need to form a search party or come all the way down to the basement. Just have the office call me next time."

"Yes, sir," said Amy. "Thank you."

I heard the door shut and Amy return to our hiding spot under the stairs. "Did you get the drone back on the shelf?" she asked.

"Almost," I replied. "I'm trying to aim the camera at the computer."

"That battery light is flashing faster," she said. She must've put her visor back on.

I made a couple more adjustments and then let the drone drop back onto the shelf. The screen tilted to the left as it settled onto the pile of cloths.

Within a few seconds, Mr. Conway entered the frame. He looked up at the lights and then over to the door.

"I forgot about the motion-sensor switch," I said.

Mr. Conway looked around the room. I didn't know if he was checking to see if anything was disturbed or if someone was hiding somewhere. Then he reached toward the drone.

"Oh no," Amy whispered.

He reached past the drone and pulled back his arm to reveal a strange device in his hand. It had a blue plastic shell and was the size of a small, thick book. A white wire was wrapped around the device. He smiled as he turned the object over in his hands.

"What is that?" asked Amy.

"I don't know," I replied.

Mr. Conway gently unwrapped the wire from around the device and moved the ends of the wires toward his ears. They were earbuds. He placed a bud into each ear and pushed a couple of huge buttons on the side of the device.

"What is that thing?" Amy asked. "That's way too big to be a phone or an MP3 player."

I didn't have an answer for her. I had never seen a machine like that before. Was it some kind of surveillance device? Was it something to sweep the room for bugs, like you see in spy movies? If it was, would he pick up the transmission from our drone?

Mr. Conway certainly didn't act like a wanted criminal. He'd been as friendly as he always was when he spoke to Amy. Although he had been surprised to see her down in the basement. Did he suspect anything? He did ask her to get the office to call him next time. Was that to keep her from coming back to the basement? To his "lair," as Sam had called it.

Mr. Conway moved to exit the room but then stopped. He turned back to the computer and reached down to touch the keyboard. It looked as if we were going to see what he was up to after all.

Then my viewscreen went dark.

"What happened?" asked Amy.

I let out a large sigh. "That's it for the battery." I pulled off my headset and tucked it into my backpack. "Come on, let's get out of here."

Once the visors and controllers were put away, Amy and I ran up the stairs, out of the basement level.

"Ask Sam to meet us in the library," I told Amy.

"The bell's about to ring," Amy replied. "Besides, she's busy making a spill in the cafeteria so I won't have lied to Mr. Conway." Amy winced. "And she's not too happy about it."

True to Amy's prediction, the bell rang. We had five minutes to get to our fifth-period classes.

"All right, everyone come up with an excuse to get out of class fifteen minutes after class starts," I said. "You got that, Noah?"

"Got it," Noah said in my earpiece.

"Sam says she will too," Amy said.

We split up and went to class. And even though engineering was my favorite subject, fifteen minutes into class I asked to be excused to go to the restroom.

The school library stayed busy throughout the day.

With so many class projects going on, students constantly filed in and out for research, so it was no big deal for four of us to gather in the back.

Noah was the last to arrive. He reached into his pocket and pulled out a granola bar, trying to open it as quietly as possible.

Amy's eyes widened when she saw it. "You're not supposed to have food in the library," she scolded.

"We didn't get to eat lunch," he said with a shrug. "All this sneaking around builds up an appetite."

"So we're not just imagining this stuff, right?" I asked. "I mean, Mr. Conway having access to the school servers and the only working school computer?"

"This better be real," said Sam. "Otherwise, I just pretended to spill soda in the cafeteria in front of the whole school for nothing." She shook her head. "I swear I heard someone say 'Soda Girl' instead of 'Water Girl.'"

Noah opened his mouth to say something but Sam shot him a glare. He took another bite of his granola bar instead.

Amy and I told them about the weird device Mr. Conway pulled from the shelf.

"Maybe it's some kind of old-school hacking machine,"

Sam said with a grin. "Maybe the tech is so old that it can't be recognized by Swift Enterprises' firewalls. That's how he gets in!"

Noah winced. "I don't think it works that way."

Sam glared at him. "Well, what do you think it is?"

Noah took another bite. "I have no idea."

"The question is, what do we do next?" asked Amy. She turned to me. "*Now* we should tell your dad, right?"

I shrugged. "We could, but . . . we still don't have any real evidence."

"Too bad the battery died," said Amy. "We could be spying on him right now."

"What if you could sneak in there and change out the battery?" asked Sam.

"Hold up," said Noah. "First of all, the basement is locked, remember? And second of all, even if we *could* sneak in, why don't we just get our drone back?"

"Dude, we have plenty of time before Friday," I said. "Don't you think it's more important to find out what Mr. Conway is up to?"

Noah shook his head. "No. I don't." He held up his hands. "Look, Tom, I know it's your dad's company and all, and I'll admit that it's been fun playing spy." He rubbed the back of his neck. "But this is really a job for the authorities, don't you think? We should just report what we know and let someone else figure it out."

"But we really don't *know* anything yet," I said.

Noah nodded. "My point exactly. There's nothing to know because nothing is going on with Mr. Conway. I guarantee it."

"You probably could've just asked for the drone if not for all this sneaking around," said Amy. "He knows most drones have cameras. If he really is a hacker, he's bound to be suspicious now."

Noah pointed at Amy. "There. See?"

"So we should *definitely* change out the battery," said Sam.

I slumped in my chair. "It doesn't really matter because we can't get into the basement anyway."

Sam smiled. "What if I had a way?"

"What are you thinking?" I asked.

"Don't ask. The less you know, the better," she replied. "But do you trust me?"

"Of course," I said.

Noah cocked his head. "When you have that evil gleam in your eye, not so much."

"Let's get back to class," Sam suggested, getting up from the table. "Let's meet here after school." She nudged Amy on the shoulder. "Amy and I will take care of getting access to the basement."

"What?" Amy asked as she got to her feet. "Why me?"

"Because you still owe me for that soda thing," Sam replied as they walked away.

"Changing out the battery, man," I said, standing up with Noah. "If Sam can really get us in . . . just think about it. Okay?"

"Yeah, all right," he said with a sigh. Then he walked out of the library.

I started to follow.

Ping. I received another text.

I stopped and checked my phone. There was another message from the unknown number. **I said to back off,** it read.

I didn't get it. If this was Mr. Conway, like Sam suggested, then why the cryptic message? It should've been more like, *Stay out of the basement.* Or, *You'll never get your drone back.* The message just didn't make sense.

I shook my head and typed back. **Who ARE you?**

I didn't expect a reply, like before. But I was wrong.

Ping.

I'm watching you, was the reply.

My head jerked up from my phone and I looked around the busy library. Students worked or spoke quietly with each other. I scanned each and every one of them. No one met my eyes. No one was watching me. But the hairs on the back of my neck stood at attention, as if someone was.

9

The Extraction Distraction

I WAS THE FIRST TO ARRIVE AT THE LIBRARY after school. Although I had two other classes with Noah, we didn't speak much. I didn't get a chance to tell him about the second text I had received. Then again, I didn't know if I would. I didn't think it would help convince him to keep the drone in the server room. And, to be honest, I was a little upset that he didn't want to help keep someone from hacking into my dad's company.

I scanned the library. There were fewer students staying after school to work on projects, but there were still enough to keep our meeting from looking out of place.

Sam and Amy entered the library. Sam wore a smug smirk, while Amy stared at her feet more than usual. Noah was right behind them. They joined me at the table near the back of the library.

"So, are you ready?" Sam beamed.

"Ready for what?" I asked.

She reached into her backpack and pulled out something thin and flat. She cupped it in her hand and placed it in the center of the table. She removed her hand and Mr. Conway's face was smiling up at me. It was his ID badge.

"What did you *do*?" I asked, covering the badge with both hands. I slid it toward me and hid it with my body.

"I said not to ask, remember?" Sam replied, giddy with excitement.

I looked around the table. Noah was speechless, eyes wide with both hands over his mouth. Amy stared at her lap, wringing her hands together. Sam grinned as she pulled her glasses off and cleaned them with the hem of her shirt. She put her glasses back on, glancing expectantly at all three of us.

Finally, she rolled her eyes. "Okay . . . ask."

"What did you . . . ?" I began.

"How in the . . . ?" Noah began.

Sam put a hand on Amy's shoulder. "Amy was amazing!"

Amy groaned. "Don't remind me." She covered her face. "I'm a thief now."

Noah and I were shocked. "Amy stole it?" I asked. "Amy?"

Sam gave Amy a playful shove. "She didn't steal anything. We're just borrowing it for a half hour. An hour, tops."

This didn't seem to make Amy feel any better. She groaned again.

Sam leaned forward. "I was the distraction," she explained. "I went up to Mr. Conway to apologize for spilling the soda, which I really did feel bad about, by the way. And while I was talking to him, Amy slipped the badge off his cart." Sam shook Amy by the shoulder. "You should've seen her. She was amazing."

"And he didn't see you?" Noah grinned and glanced at Sam and me. "Wow."

"I've always been very good at not being noticed." Amy sighed. "It's a gift."

Noah laughed. "So you decided to use your powers for evil instead of good?"

Amy groaned again and dropped her head to the tabletop. "I can't believe you talked me into this." She bumped her forehead on the table a couple of times.

I uncovered the badge and turned it over in my hands. The entire thing was a slim plastic case that held Mr. Conway's ID badge on one side and the security key card on the other.

"Come on," said Sam. "Let's go change out the battery. We may be able to get this back to him before he notices it's missing."

Noah stood. "The heck with that, let's get our drone back."

I stood and slid the badge into my hip pocket. "Come on, man. We need to see what's going on in there."

Amy shook her head without lifting it from the table. "I can't add breaking and entering to my rap sheet, guys."

"Technically it's just entering at this point," said Sam. She patted Amy on the back. "They can handle this. We'll just find out where Mr. Conway is to make sure he's not already in the basement."

Amy dragged herself to her feet. "So I'm a lookout now, huh?" she asked. "Is there no end to my life of crime?"

"Earpieces in phones, guys," Sam said as she pulled Amy out of the library. Sam seemed absolutely giddy. I had no idea she had such a devious side.

"Come on, Tom," said Noah. "Let's just get the thing out of there."

"What do you think Mr. Conway's going to think when the drone just suddenly vanishes?" I asked.

"He probably forgot all about it," Noah replied. "Just something he found and set on an old shelf. I bet he finds tons of stuff around the school."

Noah had a point. If Mr. Conway *wasn't* a notorious hacker then he probably wouldn't notice. We could just drop all of this and get back to school, back to our invention. But what if Conway really was Shadow Hawk? What if he was already onto us somehow and was sending those texts to me? He'd probably forgotten all about the drone, making it our secret weapon. We couldn't let that go to waste.

"I'll make a deal with you," I said accordingly. "We sneak into the basement and look around. If we don't find anything suspicious, we get the drone and get out of there."

Noah squinted. "Really?"

"Really," I answered.

"Deal," said Noah. "Let's go."

We pulled out our phones and connected them to our earpieces as we headed toward the stairs. Sam called me and Amy called Noah. We were now in constant contact as we made our way toward the stairwell.

We slowed as we reached the bottom of the stairs. The last thing we wanted to do was run into Mr. Conway as he entered or exited the basement. Everything was quiet, so we kept going to the bottom.

"Wait a minute," Noah said as he stepped off the last stair. "Why are we being so cautious? We have his key card. He can't get into the basement."

I put a finger to my lips in reply. Then I took that finger and pointed at the security door—actually, *beside* the door. "There's a keypad beside the card reader," I whispered. "I'm sure he knows the code if he ever loses his key card."

Noah cringed. "Right."

We crouched under the stairs and waited. Mr. Conway might already be in the basement, so we weren't making a move until we heard otherwise.

"Got him," Sam's voice said in my earpiece. "His cart is outside the second-floor boys' bathroom. I hear noises in there so I bet he's cleaning it. You'll excuse me for not checking it out personally."

"No problem," I replied. "I'm sure that's him."

"She find him?" whispered Noah.

I gave him a thumbs-up. "Let's go."

We left the stairs and crossed to the security door. Looking through the glass window, the hallway beyond seemed deserted. I dug out the key card and placed it flat on the reader. The tiny red light turned green and the lock disengaged with a small *click*. Noah pulled the door open.

We crept down the hallway. The main hall was as long as the ones in the floors above but didn't have as many doors. We slowly opened the first door we came to. The room was pitch-black beyond the threshold. Then I remembered the motion-sensor switch from before and reached in and waved my arm around. The lights flickered on to reveal a large storeroom packed with storage boxes and old equipment.

The next room was heating and air-conditioning. The room roared with the large cooling unit, and huge vents extended from machines and crisscrossed around the room.

My heart was racing. Even though the lighting wasn't as bright on the lowest level, it felt as if Noah and I were in the spotlight. We were alone in the wide corridor and I felt very exposed. We hadn't seen anyone but Mr. Conway go down to the basement, but that didn't mean he was the only one with access. For all I knew, every one of the faculty members had access through the security door. It wasn't like we had twenty-four-hour surveillance on the basement entrance. We didn't know who else came down here on occasion. If someone entered the basement while we were down there, we would have very little time, if any, to find a place to hide. We kept out of the center of the hallway just in case. Even though the temperature was cool, beads of sweat began appearing on my forehead.

We came across another storeroom, and then we opened a door and were hit with a wall of cold air. I reached into a chilled, dark room and waved my arm. The lights snapped on to reveal a familiar setting.

"This is it," I told Noah.

The room looked just like it did in the video, but I wasn't expecting the sound and temperature difference. The small space was filled with the white noise of fans cooling the server farm. There was also a deeper rumble coming from behind the small closet door. I didn't know what the door was when I saw it on video but I figured it out now.

"It's freezing in here," Noah said over the whirring fans.

I opened the door to confirm my suspicions. "The servers have their own air-conditioning unit." I pointed to the machine that nearly filled the small closet-like space. "To cool them."

"Of course," Noah replied. He turned and spotted the drone. "There it is."

As Noah grabbed the drone, I moved to the small computer desk. Just as before, the geometric screen saver animated the screen. I tapped the space bar and the shapes disappeared. The school's log-in page appeared in its place.

"Isn't that suspicious?" I asked Noah. "Every computer tied into the school system is offline but this one."

Noah shook his head. "Maybe it's not part of the system."

I pointed to the screen. "It has the school's log-in screen."

Everyone knew that the Swift Academy faculty

members had their own user names and passwords to log in to the system.

Then I noticed something tucked under the keyboard. I pulled out two colorful slips of paper. They were entry tickets to something called none other than "Hackapalooza."

I held up the tickets triumphantly. "Dude. I mean, come on."

Noah barely registered the tickets. "Yeah? So?" he asked. "I'm going to that next month too."

I waved the tickets. "You don't think this is enough evidence for our deal?"

"What, just because it has 'hack' in the name?" asked Noah. "It's a programming convention. Mostly about games and stuff. It's no big deal."

I sighed. "Look. I thought it was a crazy idea that Mr. Conway was this Shadow Hawk guy," I admitted. "I really did. And maybe he's not. But you have to admit that everything we've seen seems a little suspicious. It certainly warrants more investigation."

"Okay, fine. I can see it," said Noah. "So tell your dad or tell the FBI. Let them do it." He clutched the drone to his chest. "But leave our drone out of it. We have too much work to do on it."

I could tell there was no convincing him. I knew my friend too well.

"All right," I said. I replaced the tickets and turned to leave. "A deal's a deal."

"Wait," said Noah. "Drop Mr. Conway's key card on the floor. He'll think it fell off here."

"Good idea." I pulled out the ID badge and placed it faceup on the floor, right where he couldn't miss it.

"Hello? Guys?" Sam's voice crackled in my ear.

"Sam?" I asked. "Can you hear me?"

Noah touched his earpiece. "Amy's trying to talk to me, but I'm only getting every other word."

"It must be interference from all the power cables on the servers," I said.

"...he's...to you...someone...him," Sam's garbled voice said.

"I didn't get that," I told her. "Say it again."

Noah's eyes widened. "Amy says Conway's coming."

"...asement...someone with him," Sam's voice said.

"Oh, man," I said. I opened the door and peeked outside. I could see Mr. Conway at the other side of the door. A tall thin man in a blue shirt stood behind him. I could just make out Mr. Conway searching through his pockets.

"Can you see him?" asked Noah.

"Yeah," I replied. "And he definitely knows he's missing his key card now."

I watched as Mr. Conway poked at the keypad beside the door. Then they walked in. I eased the server room door shut. My heart raced.

"They're coming," I said. "We have to hide."

Noah glanced around and shook his head. "Where?"

I scanned the room. The racks of servers were too close to the wall to hide behind. The shelves were too full to hide on or under. That just left one place.

I opened the door to the air-conditioning unit. "In here."

Noah shook his head. "How are we going to fit in there?"

"We will," I replied. "Put the drone back and come on."

Noah held the drone tighter. "No way."

"You want him to find it missing *while* we're still here?" I asked.

Noah thought about it for a second—way too long, if you ask me—and then finally put the drone back on the shelf. Then we both backed into the small closet. My back pressed against the air-conditioning unit and Noah pressed against me. It was a really tight fit.

"Close the door," I told Noah.

"I'm trying," he said.

His body pushed against mine as he pulled the door shut. He got it to latch on the third try.

The roar of the unit was deafening. It was so loud that I couldn't hear when Mr. Conway and the other man entered the server room. I could only tell they were inside when they began speaking.

"There it is," Mr. Conway said. "I'm always losing . . ." And that's all I got. I assumed that he had just found his key card.

I strained to listen over the roaring unit, but I heard only murmurs and the occasional laugh. Every now and then I could make out familiar phrases like "Swift Enterprises," "virus," and "firewall."

It sounded as if Mr. Conway had an accomplice. Noah was closer to the door. Maybe he could make out more of what they were saying.

I didn't know how long we could stay cooped up in such a tight space. I've never been claustrophobic but I could see how it could get to some people. I could see even more so now. I tried not to think about it. Instead I concentrated on making out what Mr. Conway and his accomplice were saying.

I heard more of the murmuring voices but nothing I could make out. And then . . . nothing at all for quite a while. I gasped when a shaft of light hit my face. I thought for sure that Mr. Conway had opened the door to discover us hiding inside. Instead it was Noah. He slowly cracked open the door to peek outside.

"Are they gone?" I whispered. Then I realized that there was no way he could hear me over the roaring unit.

Noah opened the door more and poked his head out. I breathed a sigh of relief when he stepped all the way out. I was right behind him. We had the server room to ourselves once again.

"Okay, two things," said Noah. "One . . ." He pointed to the air-conditioning closet. "I don't ever want to do that again."

"Agreed," I said.

"And two . . ." He snatched the drone off the shelf. "We have to replace this battery and put it back."

"Really?" I asked. I dug into my pocket to retrieve the fresh battery.

"Yeah, Tom." Noah nodded. "I didn't catch everything, but they were talking about Swift Enterprises and its security. I think . . . I think they're both in on it."

10

The Communication Escalation

"TOM?" SAM ASKED THROUGH MY EARPIECE. "Are you there?"

"We're here," I whispered as we left the server room. "Where's Mr. Conway?"

"He and that guy are now in the computer lab," she replied.

"Let's get out of here," said Noah. "Amy's coming to meet us."

We jogged through the hallway and I saw Amy run down the stairs as we approached the security door. She ran up to the door and punched a code into the keypad outside. The door unlocked and we stepped out.

"If you knew the code, why did you swipe the key card?" asked Noah.

"I didn't before," Amy replied. "I followed Mr. Conway down and I watched him enter it. Eight-three-eight-four, by the way."

"Cool." Noah grinned. "When all this is over, we can get our drone back."

"How did you keep from getting caught down there?" Amy asked.

Noah and I exchanged a look. "That's another one of those the-less-you-know-the-better things."

The three of us ran upstairs and met Sam on the first floor.

"Is everything set?" she asked.

"The hacker tracker is good to go," said Noah.

"Hacker tracker?" I asked. "What are you talking about?"

"That's what I'm calling our drone," Noah replied.

"Oh, so now you're all on board?" asked Sam. "I thought you didn't believe Conway was Shadow Hawk."

Noah raised his hands. "And I still don't know for sure. But I heard that guy with him mention Swift

Enterprises' security system and something about the computer virus. I don't know what they're up to, but they sure weren't in there talking about custodial stuff."

I smiled and nodded. "Okay, then. Let's get here early tomorrow and see what the . . . hacker tracker picks up."

"We can see what they're up to in the computer lab right now," said Sam.

I looked around. The school was nearly deserted by this time. "I think it'll be pretty obvious if we're snooping now."

"Yeah, all right," said Noah. He pulled out his phone and began to type. "I'll text my mom for a ride." He looked up. "You all need a ride, too?"

"Yeah, sure," said Amy and Sam.

"I'm good," I said. "My dad's just next door. I told him I was staying late, so he's working late."

The three of them took off and I dug my phone out to text my dad. Before I did, I seriously wondered if I should tell him about what we had discovered. After all, this was the security of his company. The bits and pieces we had picked up were enough to pique Noah's interest. But was there enough for my dad to take seriously? And to tell him what we had learned so far, I would have to tell him everything we did to get that information: "borrowing" Mr. Conway's badge, sneaking into the basement past a security door, eavesdropping in the server room. We looked more like criminals than Mr. Conway. There was no way to get away with all that stuff without solid proof.

Then again, for all I knew, Mr. Conway and his accomplice could be stealing company secrets right now. Maybe I should just swing by the computer lab and check up on them. If I was careful, they wouldn't even know I was there.

Ping.

My phone chimed in my hand. I glanced down and saw that I had received another mystery text.

Why are you still in school, Tom? the text asked.

Ping.

I told you to let it go.

Ping.

You're going to be sorry.

I looked up from my phone and scanned the hallway. I was completely alone. How did this person know I was still here?

Then I saw something.

A figure peeked around the corner at the end of the

hallway. I froze. Was that Mr. Conway? The height was about right but I couldn't make out the face from this distance. The person was hidden behind the corner.

My heart pounded as I stared at the mystery figure. I didn't know what to do. Was I busted? Was it Conway, and he'd been onto us the entire time? If so, why the weird taunting-text game?

This person obviously knew who I was. There was no point in holding back. I gathered my courage and took a step forward.

"Hey!" I shouted. "Who are you?"

The figure ducked back behind the corner.

"Wait!" I shouted, running after the mystery person.

I made it to the end of the hall and turned toward the stairs. I heard footsteps from above, so I followed. I dashed up the stairs and spotted the person running down the second-floor hallway. He wore a hooded sweatshirt and jeans. I couldn't see who it was, but the body shape didn't match the heavyset Mr. Conway or the tall, thinner man I had glimpsed in the basement.

There was a *third* hacker? This was a bit overwhelming. How many people were in on this conspiracy?

I had to know who else was in on this. I poured on the speed and almost forgot that the computer lab was just on the left.

"What's going on out there?" Mr. Conway asked from inside the lab.

I slid to a stop and nearly stumbled as I spun around. I darted back to the stairs. I made it back to the first floor when I heard footsteps above me again. Great. Not only would I not identify the mystery person, but now I also had to dodge Mr. Conway.

I sprinted down the first-floor hallway. Luckily, the floor was completely empty. Nothing more suspicious-looking than a kid running from authority figures.

I ran to the first classroom I came to. The door was locked. I scrambled to the next one. It was locked too. Mr. Conway's footsteps grew louder and I knew there was no way I was getting to the end of the hallway before he made it to the first floor. I tried the third door—my first-period algebra classroom.

It was open!

I slipped inside and pulled the door closed behind me. I crouched and quietly turned the lock just to be sure. I stayed motionless as the footsteps grew closer.

I held my breath as Mr. Conway jogged by. When the footsteps were gone I breathed again.

"You're a bit early for tomorrow's class, aren't you, Mr. Swift?" asked a voice behind me.

I almost yelped in surprise as I spun around. My legs flew out from under me and I slumped to the floor.

Ms. Talbot sat at the teacher's desk. Her hands were poised over the computer keyboard and she glared at me over the rims of her glasses.

"Oh, I—" I stammered, scrambling to my feet. "I was just . . ."

"What?" she asked. "Playing hide-and-seek with your friends? Aren't you a little old for that sort of thing?"

"Well, uh . . ." My mind raced for something to say. "Actually, I was . . ."

Ms. Talbot smirked. "I suppose when your name is on the school you can get away with all sorts of things."

I frowned. If this lady weren't a substitute teacher then she would know things were the exact opposite. When I first attended this school, it was all I could do to prove that I wasn't going to get special privileges because there was a "Jr." at the end of my name. Sure, I get access to some of the equipment at Swift Enterprises (as long as it's not classified), but so do some of the other students—and not just the ones whose parents work there. That was the great thing about this school. I opened my mouth to protest but Ms. Talbot cut me off.

"Tell you what," she said. "I'll forget I saw you if you'll forget that I was here." She pointed to the mound of folders and books on the desk. "And the fact that I'm woefully unqualified to teach algebra. I've had to stay late just to familiarize myself with Mr. Jenkins's lesson plan."

I wanted to argue, I really did. I wanted to let her know that I don't get special treatment from anyone. But a little voice in the back of my head told me to let it go. I was getting a pass on this one. I wouldn't have to lie and make up some lame excuse about running through the halls. I could just walk out of there and Mr. Conway wouldn't know it was me he was chasing.

I bit my lower lip. Yeah, I was really tempted.

"Okay, thanks," I said finally.

I unlocked the door and left the classroom. I walked out of the school with my pride a little tarnished as I texted my dad for a ride.

11

The Incursion Inversion

"SO THERE ARE *THREE* HACKERS IN ON THIS?"
asked Noah.

"It seems like it," I replied.

We sat alone in algebra class the next morning. We were so early that we were the only ones there.

The four of us had agreed to get to school early to spy on the server room. Noah and I had texted each other, coming up with some modifications to the hacker tracker. First of all, Noah had worked on a new controller. He had boosted its range so we wouldn't have to hide under the basement stairs. With Noah's new controller, we would be able to operate the drone from anywhere in the school. The interference from the servers wouldn't be a problem.

I, on the other hand, had come seriously close to telling my father. The thing that finally stopped me was the same reason as before—lack of physical evidence. So I decided to modify a computer tablet to not only see what our VR headsets saw, but also to *record* what we saw. I connected it to an external hard drive to hold all the video data. We now had a couple of terabytes to hold evidence against Mr. Conway or Shadow Hawk or whoever he was, *and* his accomplices.

Sam and Amy entered the classroom. "I saw Mr. Conway out in the hall," Sam said as she set her backpack on her desk.

"Good," I said. "That will give us time to reposition the drone for the best view of the computer screen." I made some final adjustments to my VR headset.

Amy sat her stuff down and joined us. "Can I copilot again?"

"Hey, that's my gig," said Noah. "It's our drone, remember?"

"That's true," I said. "But Amy was great last time."

Noah pointed to the tablet. "Yeah. But we're recording everything now," he said. "We don't need a photographic memory."

Amy, Sam, and I exchanged glances.

"I really think you should let her do it, man," I said.

"Why?" asked Noah.

"He's trying to tell you that we don't need one of us throwing up during the mission," Sam said.

Noah shook his head. "It's gonna be like that, is it?"

"Please," Amy pleaded. "It was so cool last time."

Noah sighed and handed her his headset. "Fine."

While she geared up, Sam and Noah crowded around the tablet.

"Let's hope the range extender works," I said. "I don't know how all four of us would fit under the stairs."

"It'll work," said Noah. "And don't remind me about cramped places."

I turned on the headset and then powered up the remote. I flicked the camera switch and the server room flickered into view.

"Told you it would work," said Noah.

"The lights are already on," Amy observed.

"Mr. Conway must've just left the basement," said Sam.

"I'm going to test the microphone," I said. I flicked another switch on the remote and the white noise of the hard-drive fans hissed through my earbuds.

"And we have sound," said Noah.

"I can barely see the computer screen from here," said Amy.

The computer screen was in the bottom left side of the footage. A blurry black shape obscured half of it. It must have been part of the dark fabric on which the drone was placed.

"Hey," Noah said. "We were in kind of a hurry to get out of there. I aimed the camera as best I could."

"Don't worry," I said. "I'll reposition it."

From our angle, I could see that no one was sitting in front of the computer. It was safe to power up the drone.

I pushed up the left joystick to engage the drone's motors. The view shifted as the drone raised an inch off the shelf. I adjusted the right joystick to rotate the drone to the left. Now the entire computer screen was dead center. I released the left joystick and the drone settled back down on the shelf.

"What's on the screen?" asked Amy. "Is that a weird screen saver?"

The computer screen was black except for lines of green type. The lines appeared row by row from the top to the bottom. When the screen was full, the type disappeared and new lines appeared from the top again.

"That's not like the one we saw before," said Noah.

"Can you zoom in on it?" asked Sam.

"This camera can't zoom," I said fixedly. "But I can move the drone closer."

I worked the controls again and the drone rose off the shelf. The computer grew in the viewscreen as the drone drifted down toward it. Having been in the server room already, it felt surreal piloting the drone there. It seemed as if I was back in that room all over again. Goose bumps raised on my skin as if I could feel the room's frigid air.

The drone hovered closer to the screen, close enough to make out what was happening.

"Dude, that's computer code," said Noah. "It's moving so fast, I can't tell if it's compiling, transferring, or encrypting data."

"We're recording, right?" I asked him.

"As soon as you turned on the camera," Noah replied.

"Good," I said. "You can analyze it later. Frame by frame if you have to."

Although all of us were decent programmers—it was one of the first classes they taught at the academy—Noah was the best programmer I knew. If anyone could make sense of the code, it would be him.

"Just hold there a few more seconds, then," Noah instructed. "I want to collect a bit more."

I let the drone hover in place for a few seconds longer.

"Wow," said Amy. "Do you think they already hacked into your father's company?"

"I don't know," I replied. "I hope not."

I felt a knot in my stomach. What if we were too late? What if they had already stolen Swift Enterprises' secrets? I could have stopped all this. I could have told my father, convinced him somehow that this was real and not some wild conspiracy. I took a deep breath and told myself that at least we now had evidence that something fishy was going on. We just had to get Mr. Conway and his accomplices on video . . . in the act.

"I'm going to put the drone back," I announced.

I pulled the drone away from the computer and made it hover higher. I wasn't a skilled enough pilot to simply back it onto the shelf the way it had flown down. I'd have to turn it to see where I was going. I nudged the right joystick to rotate the drone to the right. A large smiling face came into view. It was the tall, thin man from the day before.

We were face-to-face with Conway's accomplice.

12

The Imminent Predicament

WE WERE STUNNED INTO SILENCE. I DON'T KNOW
about everyone else, but I froze as if the man in the
server room could actually see me. He stared directly
into the camera, so it felt as if he were looking right into
my eyes. I held my breath.

"What have we here?" the man asked, his voice coming through my earbuds. He pointed to the drone. "I see
you have a directional microphone there so I'm betting
that you can hear me."

Now I really did feel as if I were in the server room

with him. The shock of being caught like that made the room feel ten degrees colder.

"Tom," whispered Noah. "What do we do?"

"I don't know, man," I whispered back.

The man cocked his head. "How long have you been spying on me?" he asked. "I wonder if you guessed what Joshua and I have been up to down here."

The man stepped forward. Instinctively I pulled the drone back, and felt myself leaning back with it.

The man grinned. "But I bet you don't know that I have a piece of equipment here that can capture your control frequency and track it back to your location."

Amy gasped. "Can he really do that?"

"Crazy hacker stuff," said Noah, his voice pitched higher than usual. "Who knows what he can do!"

The man took another step forward and I edged the drone back.

"Of course, I'll have to crack open your drone first," the man said. "Pull out the components I need."

"Whoa, whoa, whoa!" shouted Noah. "Do *not* let him break our drone, Tom!"

The man inched forward again. I was about to move

the drone back again when he lunged at it. I threw the joystick back and the drone flew backward, just beyond his grabbing hands.

"Back wall, back wall," Sam said.

I saw the back wall loom closer in the rear camera. I released the joystick just before the drone slammed into it. The man was still coming so I increased power. The drone rose up toward the high ceiling, just out of his reach.

I aimed the microphone back at the man. "Of all the stupid, idiotic things!" He leaped into the air and grabbed for the drone. We were just out of reach.

"How long will that fresh battery last?" asked Sam.

"Not forever," Noah answered. "Four motors running simultaneously, transmitting video *and* audio. These batteries are made light as it is. They aren't built for long flights."

The man glanced around the room. He grabbed a broom from the corner and spun it around.

"He's got a broom! He's got a broom!" Noah warned.

"I see it," I said through gritted teeth.

I jerked the joystick hard to the left as the man swiped at the drone. The broom head seemed to miss the drone by inches. The view wobbled as the air current from the near miss destabilized the drone a bit.

He swung the broom again, going high. I dropped the drone just in time and the broom flew by overhead. The man put so much force into the blow that he spun around, almost falling down.

"This is nuts," I said. "I don't know how long I can keep this up."

The server room wasn't the biggest place to begin with. There were only so many times I could dodge his attacks. And if I got the drone backed into a corner, it would be dead.

The man regained his balance and began stabbing at the drone. The short jabs were harder to anticipate—all I could do was try to get away. I began backing up the drone, nearing the rear wall again. Soon, I would run out of maneuvering room.

I tried to not think about my sweaty palms slipping on the controller grips or my shaking hands flubbing the joystick. I clenched my teeth and concentrated. I had to keep everything smooth and steady.

Suddenly, the door swung open. Mr. Conway's eyes widened as he took in the surreal scene. "What in the world . . . ?" he asked.

Distracted, the other man turned to look at Conway. I flew straight toward the custodian at full speed.

"Hey!" Conway shouted as he ducked out of the way.

"Close the door!" the other man ordered.

It was too late. The drone flew over Mr. Conway's head and into the hallway. I banked left and soared down the long corridor.

"How are you going to get out?" asked Sam. "There's the security door."

I had forgotten about that. I just saw an opening and went for it.

"What's the combination again?" asked Noah.

"Eight-three-eight-four," replied Amy.

I heard rustling nearby. "Just keep them busy," said Noah's receding voice as he ran out of the classroom.

The drone reached the end of the hallway and the locked security door. I spun it around to face Conway and Broom Man.

"That . . . thing's been spying on us!" said the man. "Don't let it get away!"

Mr. Conway glanced around and shrugged his shoulders. "There's nowhere for it to go."

"We'll see about that," I mumbled.

I felt way more confident flying in the open hallway. After all, I had already piloted a high-speed drone chase through hallways full of students. This would be like the casual mode of a video game compared to that.

I jabbed the joystick forward and the drone flew right at them. Mr. Conway tentatively raised his hands but Broom Man was ready. He snarled as he held the wooden broomstick like a baseball bat.

I aimed the drone for Broom Man's face. It was as if he and I locked eyes as he grew larger in the viewscreen. Then, just as he swung the broom, I cut the power by half. The drone dropped and the broom swiped above it.

"Sa-wing, batta!" said Sam.

Mr. Conway had to duck to keep from being hit by the broom. With Conway in a crouch, I throttled up and put the drone into a steep climb. It soared over the custodian's head.

"Whoa," said Amy.

"Are you okay?" I asked. "Motion sickness?"

Amy laughed. "No way! This is amazing."

I spun the drone around to face the two men. I slowly backed it away as Broom Man inched closer.

"You know they're blocking the only way out, right?" asked Sam.

"Yeah," I agreed. "But I didn't want them to see this."

In the background, I spotted Noah through the security door window. He punched in the code and slowly opened the door. The two men didn't notice him. Then Noah slid a nearby trash can and propped the door open. He ran back up the stairs.

Sam giggled. "Way to go, Noah!"

"Can you get past them again?" asked Amy.

"I did it once, didn't I?" I asked.

Just then, Mr. Conway ducked into a nearby room. Now there was only the other guy.

I smiled. "Even easier," I said, inching the drone forward.

Then Mr. Conway emerged holding two more brooms and a mop. "Here," he said, handing the mop to Broom Man.

Both men held up their cleaning implements above their heads and began waving them about. They slowly moved forward.

"Oh boy," I said.

I brought the drone to a halt. I didn't know how I

was going to get past them now. I backed the drone away from the approaching men.

"What are you going to do?" asked Amy.

"Come up with a plan," I replied.

"What's your plan?" asked Sam.

"I don't know! I haven't come up with it yet!" I replied.

It looked as if my system of coming up with a plan on the fly was not going to work this time. I had no idea what I was going to do. I scrambled for some semblance of a plan, grasping at straws as the two men inched forward.

to fl
able

13

The Malfunction Maneuver

AS I CONTINUED TO MOVE THE DRONE DOWN THE hallway, I heard Noah run into the classroom. "Are you out yet?" he asked.

"Far from it," replied Sam. "Look."

"Are you kidding me?" asked Noah. "How are you going to get past all that?"

Sam swallowed. "I . . . I don't think he is."

Noah groaned. "Our drone is *so* dead."

It really looked like we were out of options. If I tried y through, it would be smashed to bits. I might be to back down the long hallway for a while. But sooner or later, the drone's battery would be dead. Dead is dead either way.

That was it!

"How does the battery look?" I asked.

"Can't you see on your viewscreen?" asked Amy. "About half power."

She was correct, of course. The little battery icon at the bottom of the screen was halfway filled in. Once it was nearly dead, it would be replaced by a blinking red light.

"No, I think it's just about gone," I said with a grin.

While I continued to crawl down the hallway, I slowly jiggled the throttle joystick. The image in my viewscreen wobbled up and down.

"What are you talking about?" asked Noah.

"I don't get it," said Sam. "Amy said you're at half power."

"That's right," I agreed. "But *they* don't know that."

I jiggled the joystick some more, all the while using less and less throttle. The drone slowly lowered to the ground.

"This is a big gamble," Noah warned.

He was right, but I didn't see any other way past

them. I decreased the throttle more and more until the drone was on the floor. I made it bounce up a few times to really sell it. I also left the propellers running, but not enough to get the drone airborne. If Noah's sound filter wasn't so good, I'm sure we could have heard the four motors pathetically winding down.

The mystery man lowered his makeshift weapons. "Ha! I knew it was only a matter of time." He aimed one of the broom handles down at the drone. "My kid has one of these. The batteries don't last so long. And you've had this in storage for a couple of days now?"

Mr. Conway nodded.

The other man crept closer, staring down at the drone. He extended the broom and gave the drone a shove. The view shifted right as the bristles nudged the camera lens.

"Tom . . . ," said Noah.

"Poker face, dude," I told him.

Mr. Conway lowered his brooms. "What are you going to do with it?"

Broom Man handed his supplies to Mr. Conway. "I'm going to take it apart and find out who's been watching us."

"*Tom!*" Noah repeated.

"Almost . . . ," I said.

Broom Man crouched in front of the drone and reached for it. I hit the throttle and the drone shot up three feet. Surprised, he fell back and landed on his butt. I poured on the speed and shot past Mr. Conway. The custodian's hands were so full that he couldn't do a thing to stop it.

"Get that thing!" Broom Man ordered.

I raced the drone down the hall, toward the open door.

"How did that door get open?" I heard Conway ask. The rear camera showed them running after the drone.

We zipped through the open doorway and up the basement stairs.

"Yes!" Noah shouted.

Amy laughed. "Amazing!"

Sam shushed her. "People are coming to class."

I flew the drone out of the stairwell and onto the first floor. Sam was right; the hallways were beginning to fill as students arrived for class.

"Don't bring it here," Noah warned. "You'll lead them right to us."

He was right. I checked the rear camera and spotted

Mr. Conway and Broom Man as they spilled onto the first floor. I turned my attention back to the front view and had to slow to a stop.

"Not now, Collin," I growled.

The Collybird was dead ahead. Its flashing lights made it look like a futuristic police car ready to pull me over for speeding.

I flew our drone forward and the Collybird did the same. I moved ours up and his matched my movements. I dropped our drone and so did he. I didn't think I could outmaneuver him the same way twice.

"Okay, Collin," I said. "I want you to meet some friends of mine."

I pulled the drone to a stop and then put it in reverse. The Collybird sped after our drone as it flew backward down the hall. Using the rear camera, I lowered the drone to fly through the crowd of students. Several of them jumped out of the way as the drone chase left the overhead airspace.

I saw a gap in the crowd, and whipped the drone to the right. I tweaked the joysticks to rotate the drone at the same time. The crowd of kids turned into a blur as the drone spun around.

"Woo-hoo!" Amy shouted. "I love this!"

Sam shushed her again.

"I think I'm going to be sick," said Noah.

"Close your eyes," I told him.

I straightened out the drone and continued weaving through the crowd. The kids parted as I flew toward Mr. Conway and Broom Man. He still had his broom but he couldn't swing it in a hallway full of kids. And now he had two drones to deal with.

I broke left and zipped around the men. The rear camera showed Collin breaking right.

"What kind of school is this?" asked Broom Man.

I hit the stairwell and flew the drone up to the second floor. The Collybird was still close behind. Collin wasn't giving up so easily this time.

Once on the second floor, I flew the drone over the students and down the hallway. I had to find another way to ditch both the men and the Collybird. This time, I flew into the cafeteria. It wasn't as crowded as during lunch, but there were still several students at tables eating breakfast. I thought about ducking the drone under one of the tables, or maybe hiding it behind the curtains of the stage at the end of the cafeteria. But I was out of

113

time. Both the Collybird and Mr. Conway burst into the large room.

The Collybird flew right at our drone. But Mr. Conway began closing the doors to the cafeteria. He was trying to trap the drone again.

Noah nudged my shoulder. "It's over, Tom."

"No way," I said. "I bet I can fly out through the kitchen, or . . ."

"No, Tom," interrupted Amy. All the joy had left her voice.

I didn't understand why they were giving up so quickly. I pushed up one side of my headset. Amy had hers completely off. Sam and Noah were no longer looking at the tablet. Sam's gaze shifted from me to someone past me.

I winced. "Oh, man."

I released the controls and removed my visor, blinking to adjust to the fluorescent lights of algebra class. Everyone in our first period was watching me. Worse than that, Broom Man stood front and center.

14

The Substitution Solution

"TOM SWIFT," THE MAN SAID. "I SHOULD'VE guessed it was you."

"Wait, you know who I am?" I asked.

"Of course. I work with your father often," he replied. "And I can see quite a resemblance in you."

"If you're such a good friend of his, then why are you trying to hack into his company?" asked Noah.

Sam addressed the students. "It's true. And we have video proof!"

The man held up his hands. "Now wait a minute, kids, I think there's been some confusion."

"We saw the code," said Noah.

The man nodded. "Well, yes, that was hacker code. And yes, what you saw was it trying to relentlessly look for flaws in the Swift Enterprises firewall. . . ."

"I knew it!" said Sam.

Broom Man reached into his back pocket. "Allow me to introduce myself. I'm Special Agent Fox, with the FBI."

Amy shut her eyes tight. "That's it. I'm going to prison."

Mr. Conway entered the classroom, a little out of breath. "Okay, whose drone was that?"

Noah and I raised our hands. Sam and Amy raised their hands too. "We helped," Sam said.

Mr. Conway pulled out a handkerchief and wiped the back of his neck. "Well, if you want it back, you can pick it up in Mr. Davenport's office. Hope you have a good story."

Agent Fox grinned. "Oh, I bet they do," he said. "They thought I was hacking into the computer system."

"What gave you that idea?" asked Mr. Conway.

My friends and I glanced at each other, embarrassed.

"Actually, we thought it was you, Mr. Conway," Sam said. "We thought you might be Shadow Hawk."

The class burst into laughter.

"Shadow who?" asked Mr. Conway.

Sam told him about the documentary we watched and how the photo of Shadow Hawk looked like a younger Mr. Conway. Surprisingly, everyone rumbled in agreement.

Agent Fox nodded. "Yeah, okay, I can see that. A little." Then he waved a dismissive hand. "But the FBI flipped Shadow Hawk years ago. He actually hacks for us now. Strictly white-hat stuff."

Amy raised her hand.

Agent Fox nodded at her. "I'm not your teacher. You don't have to raise your hand, Miss . . ."

"Hsu," Amy said. "Amy Hsu. I was just wondering why Mr. Conway's computer was the only one that worked in the whole school." She looked down at her lap and shrugged. "That's also why we kind of suspected him."

"It still worked because it wasn't turned on when the virus hit," Mr. Conway replied. "And it's not my computer. It's just one tied to the servers."

"Let me guess, you saw all this from your drone?" asked the agent.

"Yeah," replied Noah. "It made perfect sense at the time."

"Then who is the hacker?" I asked.

"We don't know yet," said the agent. "But we're close to finding out. The main attack at the firewall began yesterday afternoon, after school."

Agent Fox's story filled in most of the blanks. Most, but not all. What if we really had caught him trying to hack into the system and he was just covering? What if he tried to confiscate the video evidence from our drone? While everything was out in the open, I decided to call him on it.

"Well, *you* were here after school," I said. "Along with Mr. Conway and your other accomplice."

Agent Fox's smile vanished. "Other accomplice?"

"The one texting me, telling me to back off," I replied.

"Yeah," Noah agreed. I can always count on him to have my back. "What about all that stuff?"

Fox and Conway exchanged a glance. The agent shrugged. "I don't know about any texts."

There was a moment of awkward silence, when a hand slowly raised in the middle of the crowd. It was Barry Jacobs. "Uh, that was me," Barry admitted.

"Barry?" asked Mr. Conway.

Barry nodded at the man. "I overheard them talking about you, thinking you were that Shadow Hawk guy. I was trying to throw them off."

"Why?" I asked Barry.

Barry shrugged. "Because . . . well, he's my dad."

"Your dad?" I asked.

Barry nodded. "He thought I would be embarrassed going to the same school where my dad was the custodian. So when he got the job here, he used a different name."

"My real name is Jacobs, just like Barry," said Mr. Conway—or Mr. Jacobs, now. "Conway was just the name of one of my favorite movie characters."

"And it doesn't embarrass me, Dad," said Barry. "I keep telling you that."

Amy's eyes lit. "*That's* why we couldn't find any trace of him online!"

"You were cyberstalking me too?" asked Mr. Jacobs.

Amy squeaked and put her head back down.

Sam adjusted her glasses and leaned forward in her chair. "Okay, okay. But then there's that weird . . . hackerbox thing you were listening to, and the Hackapalooza tickets."

Mr. Jacobs shook his head. "Boy, you kids were all up in my business. First of all, those tickets were supposed to be a surprise. Surprise, Barry."

"Sweet," said Barry. The class laughed.

Mr. Jacobs reached into his pocket. He pulled out the book-size machine. "And this is for listening to my tunes."

"What *is* that?" asked Jessica Mercer.

"It's an antique piece of technology you little geniuses are probably unfamiliar with," he explained. "It's called a . . . Walkman."

"It's huge," said Kent Jackson. "How many albums does it hold?"

Mr. Jacobs pressed a button on the side and a small hatch opened. He pulled out a white cassette tape. "Just one at a time." He replaced the cassette and slapped it shut. "Dexys Midnight Runners doesn't sound rad without some tape hiss in the background."

You know, I was sitting with a room full of actual geniuses in one of the most advanced schools in the country, and I don't think any of us understood a word he had just said.

"Okay, *that* embarrasses me," said Barry.

The whole class laughed, and the bell rang for the beginning of class.

As everyone settled into their seats, I shook my head in disbelief. The entire thing was ridiculous, actually. My friends were some of the smartest kids in the school and we had gotten each and every clue wrong. We made up this grand mystery and spied on what we thought was the perfect perpetrator. We were completely and utterly wrong. I had to admit, I felt a little discouraged by the whole thing.

Except . . .

We might have created our own perp but we didn't create the crime. Someone really *was* trying to hack into Swift Enterprises. That part was real. And even though we hadn't discovered who did it, neither had the FBI. Fox was still searching for the actual hacker.

"I think I know who it is," I muttered.

"What?" asked Amy.

"I think I know who the hacker is," I said louder.

The class grew quiet.

Agent Fox leaned over. "What did you just say?"

"You said that the hacker started the main assault on the servers after school yesterday, right?" I asked him.

Fox nodded. "That's right."

"Well, Ms. Talbot was working late yesterday too," I said.

"Talbot?" asked Agent Fox. He glanced at Mr. Jacobs. "Who's that?"

"She's our substitute for this class," I replied. "I saw her here yesterday afternoon." I pointed to her desk. "And she was working on that computer. Not her laptop, like before. The school computer."

Mr. Jacobs went to the front of the class and tapped on the space bar. The school's log-in page appeared. "Hey, this computer wasn't off, it was in standby mode."

"Let me see that," said Agent Fox. He sat at the desk and entered a username and password. He must have been given one for the investigation. After a brief delay, a familiar line of code began filling up a black screen.

Agent Fox stood. "Where is Ms. Talbot now?"

"She's been two and a half minutes late for the past two days," Amy reported. "Give or take thirty seconds. She should be showing up right about . . . now."

Ms. Talbot entered the classroom. "Sorry I'm late again. I just can't seem to . . ." Her voice trailed off as she saw all the staring faces. Her eyes fell on Agent Fox. "What?"

15

The Custodial Confinement

"I KNOW MANY OF YOU ACTUALLY SAW OUR hacker tracker in action a few days ago," I said to the audience. "Some a *little* closer than others." A ripple of laughter rolled through the cafeteria. "But none of you got to see it from the pilot's perspective."

"I think you'll get a better idea of the prototype's unique maneuverability and audio recording capabilities," Noah added. "Plus, it's way cool."

I motioned to Amy in the back of the cafeteria. "So if we can kill the lights"—Amy flipped off the lights—"here is what *we* saw that day."

We left the stage as the large projection screen filled with the scene from the server room. We were playing back the entire video we recorded during the chase. It was our grand finale for our demonstration at this month's invention convention.

We joined Amy in the back just as the drone's view shifted dramatically. Noah saw the shift and shut his eyes.

"You do realize," he said, "that if someone gets sick in here, we're probably going to be the ones cleaning it up."

I sighed. "Yeah, I know."

He was right. After Agent Fox had taken away Ms. Talbot in handcuffs, Noah, Amy, Sam, and I went straight to Mr. Davenport's office and told him everything. And I mean everything—every sneak, ditch, and steal (uh, borrow).

Our principal was not happy at all. Even though our actions helped find the hacker in the end, we were still disruptive to the school. He gave us our drone back, but he sentenced us to one month's community service . . . in the custodial department. That's right, we are Mr. Jacobs's assistants every day before and after school and after lunch. Now we *all* have the basement passcode memorized.

Finding the hacker went a little further with my father, but not by much; he grounded me for two weeks. My dad was more upset that I didn't tell him our suspicions in the first place. Even though our theory about Mr. Jacobs was disproved, my dad wanted me to know that I could always come to him about anything; that it won't matter how crazy or outlandish my theories may seem. We'll see how that goes. With the way my mind works, I have got some . . . unconventional ideas, to say the least.

"This is my favorite part," Amy said, pointing to the screen. It was the part where the drone flew out of the basement hallway and up the stairs.

Noah groaned.

"Why do you look?" I asked him. "I mean, really."

"Because it's supercool," he replied. "And I'm trying to toughen up."

"Keep trying," I said.

"I talked to Collin, and he's going to teach me how to fly his drone," Amy said. "And if I'm good enough, I want to get my own and help him patrol the halls."

"An Amybird?" Noah asked.

Amy didn't take the bait. "Yeah, isn't it great?"

I scanned the room. "Where's Sam?" I asked. "Didn't you say she was going to enter something after all?"

Amy looked around. "That's what she said. Maybe she changed her mind. Too much pressure."

"Did she tell you what it was?" I asked.

Amy shook her head. "She said it was a surprise. She said she got the idea from our hacker tracker mission."

"Oh yeah?" asked Noah. "As long as it's not a new dating app."

It turned out that Mr. Jenkins had really been sick. I heard from my dad that Ms. Talbot (or whatever her real name is) hacked a dating app so she could be matched with Mr. Jenkins. They went on a date and she slipped something into his food. I guess Agent Fox will have to add poisoning to her list of crimes.

The video was now at the part where the drone flew into the cafeteria. Mr. Jacobs shut the doors while the Collybird circled. The view shifted when our drone floated to the ground and the screen went blank.

The audience applauded and Noah switched on the lights. "You're lucky I wrote that soft-landing protocol into the drone for when someone releases the controls."

"Hey, what was I supposed to do?" I asked. "FBI agent, right in front of me."

"You didn't even know he was an agent yet," Noah said.

"Exactly!" I shook my head. "I thought he was a bad guy."

Amy shushed us. "Guys. It's Sam."

Sam stood on the stage next to Mr. Edge, the monthly host of the invention convention. There was a table with a black cloth hiding something underneath.

Mr. Edge took the microphone from the stand. "Our final exhibition for this month comes from . . . Samantha Watson!"

The audience clapped as she took the microphone.

"Hello," she said nervously. "This isn't the most life-changing invention, but I think it can be pretty useful." She bumped the microphone as she tried to remove the cloth from the table. "Sorry. I was up late building the prototype. I took apart my phone to do it, which my parents weren't happy about. . . ."

The audience laughed.

Sam removed the cloth to reveal something very familiar. It was a mock-up of a key card reader attached to a small door.

"Okay, here it goes." She picked up a plain plastic card. "We've all seen these, right? A security key card. You hold it up to the reader and . . ."

Sam held the card to the reader and the red light turned green. There was a loud *click*. She turned the handle on the small door and it opened.

". . . there you go." She turned to Mr. Edge. "If I can have a volunteer from the audience."

Mr. Edge joined her onstage and she handed him the card.

"If someone steals or 'borrows' your key card, they can get in too, right?" she asked.

Amy made a little squeaking noise.

Sam nodded at Mr. Edge, and the teacher pressed the card to the reader and the light turned green again. Sam opened the unlocked door. Then she picked up another card from the table. It was black and had a white circle on one end.

"But this key card only works for me," she explained. "It's the same size and shape as a normal key card. That was the hard part. But it reads *my* thumbprint."

She held the key card against the reader and the light turned green. She opened the tiny door again.

"It won't work for anyone else." She handed the black card to Mr. Edge.

The teacher tried the card, holding it several different ways, and the light stayed red. He handed it back to Sam and she placed her thumb back in the circle. When she held the card against the reader, the light turned green again.

"And that's it," she said.

The students applauded as Mr. Edge took the microphone back.

"Great job, Samantha," he said. "And great job to all our inventors. See you next month!"

We were still clapping when Sam joined us in the back. Noah even threw in a couple of whistles.

"What did you think?" she asked. "It's no big water project but . . ."

"Are you kidding?" I asked. "That was great."

"Simple, elegant, the best," Noah added.

Amy grabbed her by both arms. "You are the best friend ever," she said. "You redeemed me. You put my criminal rampage to good use."

"Yeah, I'm going to need one of those," said a voice behind us. It was Mr. Jacobs.

Amy cringed. "I'm sorry, I'm sorry, I'm sorry."

Mr. Jacobs laughed. "I already told you, Amy, don't worry about it." He handed out a couple of push brooms. "Besides, it got me help for a whole month. I might actually take a vacation for once."

We already knew the drill. Noah and I fold and roll away the tables while Sam and Amy sweep up the trash and bits of food. Then . . . everybody mops.

"Man, since when did kids get so sloppy?" Noah asked as he rolled away a table.

I shook my head. "Okay, are you going to ask that every day?"

"Yeah, probably," Noah replied.

Sam glided by with her push broom. "I think I'm beginning to identify students by the crumbs they leave behind. Gross."

"Oh, I figured that out the second day," Amy chimed in. She pushed her broom in the opposite direction and shook her head. "Photographic memory. A blessing and a curse."

The rest of us cracked up. Only twenty-seven more days of this to go. It was a lot of work, but as punishments go, it could've been worse.

DON'T MISS TOM'S NEXT ADVENTURE!

- The Sonic Breach -

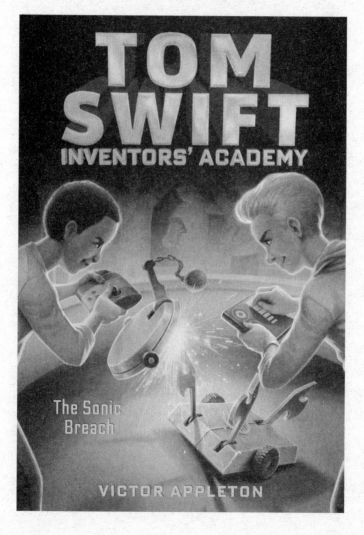

The Conjunction Malfunction

"YOU'RE GOING DOWN, WATTS," NOAH SAID TO his opponent.

"Bring it, Newton," Jamal Watts replied.

The two faced off inside a circle of other students. And no, this wasn't some kind of after-school fight. It wasn't even after school. This was during our robotics class, and the two combatants weren't combatants at all. A large robot rested on the floor beside each of them.

One of the cool things about attending the Swift Academy of Science and Technology is that you never knew what the day might have in store. Sure, most schools held field trips to local museums, but Swift Academy students might get to work on a project with NASA. Regular schools might have well-equipped science departments. But the academy students have access to a lot of the high-end equipment at the next-door Swift Enterprises—a major government contractor.

Or, we could keep it simple like today and have a robot battle sparring session in part of the gym during robotics. All right, there were several cool things about our school.

"Okay, teams," Mrs. Scott said with a smirk as she strolled to the center of the circle. Her usual red bandanna held back her curly jet-black hair. Usually dressed in overalls, she always looked like someone who grew up in a mechanics shop. And judging by the wrench tattoo peeking out from her rolled-up shirtsleeve, she probably did. "Enough trash talk. Final checks."

This year, Mrs. Scott had us build robots for our very own robot battle—just like the ones you see on television. She had outlined the specifications for the robots, and we divided into teams to build one of our own. Luckily, I got to work with my friends Noah Newton and Samantha Watson.

Noah worked the joysticks on his controller. Our robot's body was half a meter square and fifteen centimeters tall. It looked like an oversize flat gift box painted battleship gray. The robot moved forward and backward as Noah controlled it. "Locomotion, check," he said.

Sam toggled the joysticks on her controller. She was in charge of the three axes protruding from the top of our robot—two in the front, one in the back. Okay, they weren't real axes—more like ax-shaped hammers with blunt edges. But I designed the heads to be shaped in such a way that they created a ramp when the front two were in the down position; the same with the one on the back. That way, our robot could not only whack an opposing robot but also wedge itself underneath the opponent. Then the axes could raise and potentially flip over the enemy.

"Axes are a go," Sam reported as the ax heads raised and lowered. Even though we had only plastic heads installed for today's practice match, a devious grin stretched across her face as she brought them down in a chopping motion.

My job was a little different. I had a tablet connected to my controller for power distribution. Noah had coded a simplistic AI for our robot. It wasn't a true artificial intelligence, but it stored several preset maneuvers. It also allowed power levels to be adjusted in real time. With a swipe on my tablet, I could give more power to the axes for attacks or flips. I could also assign all power to the drive motor for a quick escape.

I checked the readings on the tablet. "AI and power levels are good," I announced.

Noah turned to me and grinned. "One final test," he said, his dark eyes gleaming through his safety goggles. "Let's hear it, Tom."

"Really?" I asked. "For a practice match?"

"Come on," Noah urged. "You know you want to."

Noah had pulled the team leader card and insisted on naming our robot. He called it the Choppa. That made sense and all; it did wield three ax-shaped hammers. But the real reason behind the name was a meme he had found on the Internet. It showed a picture of Arnold Schwarzenegger standing in a jungle, muscles rippling and covered in sweat and camouflage face paint. Under the image were the words *GET TO THE CHOPPA!* Noah liked the meme so much that he talked us into pasting the image on the top of our robot.

"Come on! Do it!" Noah growled in his best Arnold impersonation. "Do it! I'm right here!"

I shook my head and pressed a button on my controller.

"Get to za choppa!" shouted Arnold's voice from a hidden speaker on our robot. "Get to za choppa!"

The surrounding students laughed. Nothing cracks up a bunch of twelve- and thirteen-year-olds like a good meme, even an oldie but a goody.

About the Author

VICTOR APPLETON is the author of the classic Tom Swift books.